The evening air was already nippy as Kylie hurried toward Main Street.

As she came around the corner, she saw Landon standing outside the restaurant. She slowed her steps even as her heart picked up speed.

She loved it when he wore blue shirts. They always made his eyes look bluer, and with his wavy dark hair, he truly was a good-looking man. A fact many of the other riders' wives and girlfriends had certainly noticed. Yet she'd never seen him flirt. Not once.

"Landon, where are your crutches?"

"I thought we were going right in to dinner so I didn't need them."

"And yet, here you are," she said, shaking her head. "Not smart."

"We can fix that. Here, put your arm around my waist," he said as he slid an arm around her shoulders and leaned against her slightly.

At first she couldn't speak. He smelled so good. Felt too good. The warmth of his body seeped into hers, beckoning her closer. He was all lean muscle. Rock solid.

"Is the leg bothering you?" she asked, tightening her arm around him.

"Not especially."

Suspicious, she looked up at him. "So why are we plastered to each other?"

Dear Reader,

Well, I must say, it feels good to be home. While this is my first Western Romance, my very first published book was with Harlequin American Romance somewhere back in the early nineties. At the time, all I read were Americans, so when I decided to try my hand at crafting a story, of course I submitted to that particular line. Oh, and by the way, writing a short book? Not as easy as I'd thought it would be. Wow, what a humbling experience!

Anyway, I wrote for American for quite a long time, with the occasional Love & Laughter, Duets or Intrigue thrown in. Then I switched to Blaze and wrote for that line for over fifteen years. When I was told I could bring my Made in Montana series with me to Western Romance, I was delighted to come full circle.

Stealing the Cowboy's Heart takes place in the fictional town of Blackfoot Falls, Montana. It's the eighteenth book in the series, but I've peppered in some of the more interesting characters as a means of introducing you to the town and its sometimes wacky, sometimes annoying townspeople, who might like to gossip a bit more than most.

I hope you enjoy Kylie and Landon's story. We all welcome you to Blackfoot Falls!

Happy reading!

All my best,

Debbi

STEALING THE COWBOY'S HEART

DEBBI RAWLINS

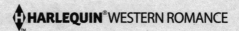

Recycling programs
for this product may
not exist in your area.

ISBN-13: 978-0-373-75778-7

Stealing the Cowboy's Heart

Copyright © 2017 by Debbi Quattrone

This edition published by arrangement with Harlequin Books S.A.

For questions and comments about the quality of this book, please contact us at CustomerService@Harlequin.com.

® and TM are trademarks of Harlequin Enterprises Limited or its corporate affiliates. Trademarks indicated with ® are registered in the United States Patent and Trademark Office, the Canadian Intellectual Property Office and in other countries.

Printed in U.S.A.

Debbi Rawlins grew up on the island of Oahu in Hawaii but always loved Western movies and books. When she was twelve she spent the summer on the Big Island of Hawaii, and had the dubious honor of being thrown off her first horse. A year later, minutes before a parade started down her street, she managed to find the most skittish horse in the lineup and...you can probably guess the rest.

These days, sixty-five-plus books later, she lives on four acres in gorgeous rural Utah surrounded by dogs, cats, goats, chickens and free-range cattle, who just love taking down her fence every couple years.

Books by Debbi Rawlins

Harlequin Blaze

Made in Montana

Alone with You
Need You Now
Behind Closed Doors
Anywhere with You
Come On Over
This Kiss
Come Closer, Cowboy
Wild for You
Hot Winter Nights
Sizzling Summer Nights

Visit the Author Profile page
at Harlequin.com for more titles.

This is for Megan and Kathleen—I bet you two were cheerleaders in high school. Am I right?

Thank you for all your patience and support, and for helping me make the transition to Western. You're both terrific!

Chapter One

"Don't get me wrong, it's a cute dress. Just kinda conservative."

Kylie Richardson glanced down at the simple blue sheath and sighed. She almost always wore jeans. She liked jeans. They were comfortable, casual, easy. Dresses always made her think of Easter and holding her stomach in. Why on earth had she agreed to go on this date? Just the thought of it made her palms clammy.

"If I were you, I'd be showing off those curves," her friend Mallory said before taking a bite of her apple fritter.

"Well, that's a nice way of putting it," Kylie said with a laugh that ended in a groan. Since moving to Blackfoot Falls, Montana, and opening The Cake Whisperer thirteen months ago, she'd gained six pounds. Obviously from enjoying too many of her own cupcakes.

Mallory stopped chewing and swallowed. "What do you mean?"

She'd moved from California and opened the bar next door about the same time and they'd become fast friends. Tall and slim with honey-colored hair that Kylie coveted with unabashed envy, Mallory didn't have to worry about indulging her sweet tooth.

The bell above the door jingled, saving Kylie from having to reply.

Aunt Sally, who owned the Cut and Curl—the only beauty parlor in town—walked into the bakery and frowned at the dress. "Oh, for heaven's sake, you still have that old thing?"

"I was hoping you didn't get that at the new consignment boutique." Rachel Gunderson, another friend who knew practically everyone within a hundred miles, entered right behind Aunt Sally. "It doesn't flatter you at all."

Kylie spotted the elderly Lemon sisters across the street, squinting and trying to see them through the window. "Lock the door, will you, Rachel?" The bakery was closed for the day but Kylie should've known better. People around their small town didn't pay any attention to signs or wait for invitations.

Usually Kylie didn't mind, and she certainly welcomed these women. Her aunt was the main reason Kylie had chosen to settle in Blackfoot Falls. But she sure didn't need any more opinions about her dress.

Rachel's attention had wandered to Mallory. "Did that just come out of the oven?"

"Tastes like it," Mallory muttered around another bite of the fritter.

"They're from this morning," Kylie said, grateful for the distraction. "I have a couple left in the back. Some scones too, I think. Go help yourselves."

Sally looked as if she was struggling with temptation. "Good Lord, girl, I don't know how you learned to bake like an angel," she said, smoothing a hand over her ample hip. This month her naturally brown hair was tinted auburn...kind of close to Rachel's color. "Your mom sure didn't teach you. That sister of mine could burn ice cream."

Rachel emerged from the back with a tray of goodies. "What about the turnovers? Are they off-limits?"

"Nope. Just forgot about 'em."

Sally sighed and snatched one with a dark golden crust. "Sassy's should still be open. Get on over there and find yourself something sexy," she said before taking a bite. "By the way, who's the lucky guy?"

"Oh, you expect me to volunteer a name?" Kylie brought out a stack of napkins from under the counter. "You really think I'm that stupid?"

"Well, I figure it's better than us asking around until we find out."

Kylie groaned.

"You know what? Sassy's is a good idea," Rachel said. "Beth Landers dropped off a bunch of clothes yesterday. Nice stuff. Some of it designer."

"Then hell yes, you'd better get over there before the Sundance guests get wind of it." Sally licked the tips of her long red-painted fingernails. "They'll be swarming the place like vultures."

Rachel chuckled. "Good point," she said, clearly taking no offense. Her family owned the Sundance. Back when the town had faced hard times, it had been Rachel's idea to turn a portion of the sprawling cattle operation into a dude ranch.

"Beth has to be five inches taller than me." Kylie was tempted, though. Beth owned a cute boutique inn on Main Street and always looked so great.

"You're close to the same size in every other way. All you'd have to do is hem," Sally said. "When's the big night? Tomorrow, right?"

Kylie nodded.

"Good. Once you find a dress, come over to the Cut and Curl. I'll put some highlights in your hair."

"Tomorrow really isn't a big deal," Kylie muttered, but couldn't help glancing longingly at Mallory, who was checking the time. Probably needed to go open the bar soon. It gave Kylie a moment to wonder if her own hair was too dark to pull off some honey-colored highlights.

"Of course it's a big deal. You waited a whole year before diving back in after you got rid of Gary. That was very sensible." Sally smiled gently. "And don't let your mother tell you otherwise. I love my sister dearly, but that woman doesn't know how to live without a man. I hope she's not still harping on you to take back that no-good cheating bum."

Heat flooded Kylie's face. The other two women knew about most of her past. But it wasn't a topic she liked discussing. Especially now that the year she'd given herself had stretched to nearly fourteen months. She wasn't ready to date. She barely even knew how. Gary had been the only guy in her life since high school.

"Hey, I'll go with you to Sassy's," Rachel said with an understanding smile.

"Oh, hell, I didn't mean to upset you, honey." Her aunt set the turnover aside on a napkin, a worried frown creasing her heavily made-up face.

"You didn't." Kylie shrugged. "I just don't want to spend money on a dress I'll probably never wear again."

"You will." Mallory wiped her hands. "Do you know how many cowboys who come to the Full Moon are dying to go out with you?"

"Oh, God." Kylie rolled her eyes. Just what she needed. Another cowboy.

Mallory grinned. "Go to Sassy's with Rachel," she said. "I'd go, too, but I have to open soon. Besides, I'm hopeless at shopping for dresses. You know me, I'm always in jeans and T-shirts."

Nodding, her mouth full, Rachel mumbled, "Just let me finish this fritter and we'll go."

Kylie glanced around her small shop. She still had to clean out the glass case and sweep and mop the floor. Get the coffee ready for tomorrow morning's rush. At least the kitchen was finished.

She looked down at her frumpy dress. It couldn't hurt to spend a few bucks on something that had been manufactured in the twenty-first century.

"Hey, where's the other turnover?" Sally asked.

Still chewing, Rachel pointed to her tummy.

Sally's eyebrows shot up. "You're kidding?"

Mallory looked surprised too, but she just laughed and headed for the door.

"Nope," Rachel said. "After all, I'm eating for two now."

Mallory's hand froze on the doorknob as she slowly turned with a shocked expression that rivaled Sally's. Kylie couldn't move at all. Neither her feet nor her mouth seemed to be working.

"You little devil." Sally rushed in and hugged Rachel so hard she started coughing. "How far along are you?" Sally drew back but held Rachel at arm's length. "For heaven's sake, hurry and finish coughing and tell us everything."

"Congratulations, Rach," Mallory said. "I'm so happy for you and Matt."

Kylie struggled to speak. Her jaw was locked shut, so she hurried into the kitchen for a glass of water. And to give herself time to slow down her heart rate and to fight back the tears that threatened to burst from her eyes.

She was happy for Rachel. Of course she was...

Rachel was a kind and wonderful person. So was her husband, Matt, and they'd been trying to get pregnant since Kylie had moved to town.

Kylie gulped down the water, then brought out another glass. She knew she was being irrational. Kylie was only twenty-six, but she'd always planned to have started her own family by now. With Gary. The lying scumbag, who for nine years had promised her a happily-ever-after. He'd painted a perfect picture. Right after he won his first big cash prize, she'd get her dream wedding. They'd have a passel of kids, with enough money to fulfill all their dreams.

She could still hear him say, "Honey, everything I do, I do for us." He'd said it so often, she should've been suspicious. Or even had a clue. Long before she'd caught him with two blondes in the bed Kylie had shared with him.

SHORTLY AFTER LANDON KINCAID crossed into Wyoming he spotted an exit sign up ahead. It was getting late, the September sun already dipping behind the Rockies in the distance. Probably about time for him to stop for the night. Too bad his mom was away visiting his sister in Salt Lake. His family's ranch, which his older brothers had been running since their dad's passing, was just over a hundred miles south. Landon figured he'd catch them on his way back.

Anyway, this exit was as good as any since he hadn't planned on driving straight through to Blackfoot Falls. His leg ached from sitting behind the wheel for the better part of ten hours. The last thing he wanted to do was to hobble out of his truck like an old man after not seeing Kylie for a whole year.

Yeah, she'd seen him in worse shape, even patched him up plenty of times in the past. But that's not why he'd been driving eleven hundred miles to see her. After she'd kicked Gary out of her life, Landon had promised himself he'd give her a year—give them both a year—before he made his intentions clear.

Tomorrow would be thirteen months and two weeks. He would've showed up sooner if he hadn't busted up his leg. Waiting had been brutal. The image of her climbing into her rickety compact on the night she'd left Iowa, the muffler about ready to fall off, had been imprinted in his mind. Her face had been blotchy, her nose red and her eyes puffy, and all he'd wanted to do was put his arms around her and hold on tight. Instead, he'd asked if he could help load her belongings.

She'd turned on him so fast, her fury tangible in the night air. He could still hear her words…

"I don't want anything to do with any of you damn cowboys. You hear me? Nothing. If you want to help, leave me alone." She'd thrown two more boxes into the car, and swung back to face him. "Everything was fine between Gary and me until you—"

She hadn't finished. Just fled to safety behind the wheel.

He'd just stood there like a helpless idiot, twisted with guilt and a deep, gut-wrenching sense of loss, trying not to feel responsible for everything that had gone wrong for Kylie those last two years, as he watched his best friend's girl drive away.

Shaking the memory off, Landon turned his truck into a motel parking lot. Hell, he didn't even remember leaving the expressway. That kind of crap had happened too many times in the past couple of months. Thoughts of seeing Kylie again, hoping she'd give him a chance to fix things, had distracted him. Cost him plenty, too.

Stopping under the flashing green Vacancy sign, he'd

planned on letting the truck idle while he dashed into the office. Naturally, his leg wouldn't cooperate. He tried flexing the muscle but it burned like hell. Impatient, he grabbed his crutches. Lately, he did okay without them… as long as he didn't overdo it. Now wasn't the time to be stupid.

After he'd registered and gotten a key, he drove across the parking lot to the gas station on the corner. All six pumps were free and he figured it was better to refuel now and leave his options open tomorrow. Hell, he might even tackle some extra exercises the physical therapist had given him.

Leaning on one crutch for support, he was halfway through filling the tank when someone pulled up next to him. He nodded at the older man getting out of his battered pickup loaded with bales of hay. Landon realized someone else was in the truck when he heard the passenger door slam.

"Hey, aren't you Landon Kincaid?" The scruffy blond kid coming around the bed looked to be in his midteens.

"Last time I checked." Landon eyed the baggy jeans and the backwards baseball cap. Not the typical rodeo fan but he obviously followed the sport. A year ago the kid probably wouldn't have recognized him.

After eight years of rodeoing, Landon had finally made it to the national finals last December. He hadn't nabbed the title, but he'd gotten close enough that fans had taken notice. So had two major sponsors. And then Landon had gone and done something stupid.

"Hey, Gramps," the boy said. "You know who this is, right?"

The man lifted the gas pump nozzle and squinted at Landon. "You gonna make it to the finals again?"

"I hope so. Or I'll die trying."

"Well, don't do that," the man said, chuckling. "You still got time. How much longer before they let you back on a bronc?"

"A couple weeks." He heard a click, added enough fuel to round up to the next dollar and removed the nozzle. Forgetting about the crutch, he almost lost his balance.

"Is that what the doc says?" The man watched the crutch bounce off Landon's truck and land on the oil-stained cement.

"Maybe three weeks," Landon muttered.

"Everybody was shocked you got thrown, even the commentators." The kid picked up the crutch and brought it to him. "Lucky that mare didn't stomp your head. I heard she missed your ear by an inch."

Yeah, tell him something he didn't already know. "Thanks," Landon said, opening his door and shoving the crutch to the passenger side.

"What happened? She get spooked?"

"Come on, Tommy," the grandfather said, giving the boy a stern look. "Leave the man alone."

Landon might've left things at that but the kid grabbed a squeegee from a bucket and started washing his windshield. "It wasn't the horse, it was me," he said, surprised by his candor. How many times had he been asked that question? And had always given the same answer...he didn't know. "I guess I let my mind wander for a second."

"Really?"

Hell, it wasn't a guess. "Not a smart thing to do with thirteen hundred pounds of bucking horseflesh underneath you."

"What were you thinking about?"

Landon snorted a laugh. "A girl."

Tommy stopped scrubbing the windshield and stared. "You serious?"

Already regretting his words, Landon pocketed the gas receipt and said, "Thanks for your help, buddy. Appreciate it."

"No problem." Tommy hurried around to wash the other side. "You got an autographed picture I could have?"

Landon shook his head. Joining the winners' circle had its drawbacks. "Tell you what. You ever come to a rodeo where I'm riding, you let me know and I'll hook you up with free tickets." He scribbled his cell number down, something else he never did and would likely regret.

"Wow. Thanks, dude." Tommy stared at the piece of scrap paper.

"You don't give that number out to anyone else, or no free tickets. Got it?"

The kid nodded. "How about a selfie?"

Landon wasn't keen on those either, but it wouldn't kill him. "All right. Just one."

"With the crutches?"

"No," he said in a tone that allowed no argument.

Tommy's grandpa chuckled. "Come on, boy. Quit bothering the man and let's go deliver this hay."

Landon grabbed his Stetson from the passenger seat and settled it on his head. Tommy got his photo and after they shook hands, Landon slid back behind the wheel. He automatically massaged his thigh muscle. It throbbed from standing just those few extra minutes. Had to be the long drive. He was getting better every day. And every one of those days counted in a big way. He couldn't afford to mess up.

A split second of inattention in the saddle had landed him on the ground, his leg broken in two places. All because he'd caught a glimpse of a woman he'd thought was Kylie sitting in the stands.

So much for his fast track to the finals in December. Oh, with his scores, he still had a good shot. But only if his leg healed soon.

He doubted Kylie had been keeping up with rodeo news. She wouldn't know he'd been winning big. Or that he'd gotten hurt. He didn't care about any of that stuff, though. What he didn't want was her thinking he needed tending. Dammit, it was long past time Kylie understood exactly what he wanted from her.

Chapter Two

Kylie took another peek at herself in the big round hand mirror sitting on the counter by the oven. She'd gotten ready at home but asked Kevin to pick her up at the bakery. If he'd thought it was weird he hadn't let on. He seemed like a very nice man, or she wouldn't have accepted his dinner invitation, but she still preferred meeting on neutral ground.

The new haircut Sally had given her had transformed her boring blunt bob to a medium shag, the layers highlighted with subtle streaks of warm caramel and dark gold. She still couldn't believe that was her hair. Or that the woman in the mirror was *her*. She hoped the makeup wasn't too much.

She still wasn't sure about the dress. The low-cut neckline would've looked a lot better on someone bustier and the short length hitting her five inches above her knee stretched the boundaries of her comfort zone.

No, she would never have chosen this dress for herself. But Rachel hadn't let her get away with anything conservative. There was even another dress that she'd insisted was perfect for Kylie, which was absolutely in no way even close to perfect, and yet it now hung in Kylie's closet.

Rachel was something else. Kylie had never had a friend like her before. Come to think of it, she hadn't had any close girlfriends. After she'd met Gary, it had been just the two of them, practically inseparable. Until he'd become obsessed with making a name for himself riding rodeo.

He'd wanted the big prize money, the gold buckle and, apparently, the many women who had no trouble undoing that buckle.

Someone knocked on the front door, despite the Closed sign. Kylie checked the time. Too early for Kevin, who'd warned her he might be a bit late because of a work emergency. He not only managed the motel in town, but also two others in Kalispell, forty-five minutes away.

Kylie shook her head as she unlocked the door for Rachel. "How did you know I'd be here?"

"Oh, my God. Your hair looks fabulous." Rachel gave her a head-to-toe inspection. "And the dress… What a great find. It couldn't be more perfect. But honestly, those highlights and that flirty cut… Sally outdid herself. I really like it."

"Flirty? Really?"

"Come on, don't you love it?"

"I do. I've wanted something different for a while now, but I should've waited."

"Why?"

"I was hoping for something subtler. Kevin will think I got all glammed up for him."

"Oh, sweetie, he won't be looking at your hair," Rachel said, grinning at the V of the dress.

"What?" Kylie tugged the neckline up.

"Stop it." Rachel swatted her hand away and made her own adjustment. "You should wear red more often. It suits you."

"Is the makeup too much? I'm a little out of practice."

"It looks great." Rachel glanced around, then sniffed

the air. "I swear pregnancy has thrown my senses out of whack. You didn't burn anything, did you?"

"This morning I was distracted and— Oh. It's me, isn't it?" Kylie frantically fanned the air. "I smell like burnt toast."

"Nope, it's not you. It's coming from the kitchen but it'll probably be gone by the time you open tomorrow."

"That doesn't help me tonight."

Rachel smiled. "It's not that strong. I'm sorry I mentioned it."

"Do you mind if we step outside so I can air out?" She paused on the way to the door. "Oh, and I have some chocolate cupcakes if you're interested."

Moaning, Rachel pressed a hand to her stomach. "Not for me, thanks. I ate like a fiend yesterday and paid dearly for it. Anyway, I've got to run over to the market so I can finish dinner. I just stopped by to make sure you wore the dress."

Kylie grinned. Knowing Rachel, she wasn't joking. "What would you have done if I hadn't?"

"That's a silly question. Made you go home and change, of course."

A maroon truck slowed, then pulled to the curb just as they stepped onto the sidewalk. The tinted windows prevented her from seeing inside.

"Is that Kevin?" Rachel asked.

"He drives a Mustang." Kylie left the door propped open. She hoped the driver was going to the Full Moon Saloon next door, and wasn't thinking the bakery was open.

"Well, I've got to scoot," Rachel said, checking her watch and backing away. "You have a good time tonight. Don't change a thing. Leave that neckline right where it is." She took a couple steps back. "Wait. Fresh lip gloss. That's all you need."

"Goodbye, Rachel," Kylie said patiently, dying to tug the dress up an inch. "Better watch where you're going."

Bumping into a parked SUV got Rachel to turn around with a startled laugh.

Kylie smiled as she watched her friend hurry across the street. Rachel wouldn't make it to the Food Mart without running into someone else to chat up. The woman knew everyone.

She and Mallory had been godsends for Kylie. Moving to a strange town where she hadn't known anyone but Aunt Sally had proved scarier than Kylie had imagined. Her new friends had made all the difference.

"Kylie?"

At the sound of the deep voice, she froze. Her heart lurched. Had to be her imagination. Resisting the urge to spin around, she turned slowly.

Landon?

Except it couldn't be...

Here in Blackfoot Falls? It just wasn't possible...

And yet she was staring at all six feet of him, leaning against the maroon truck, hat in hand, wearing his usual jeans and scuffed boots, his brown hair in need of a trim. Although it tended to look like that all the time, even after he'd gotten it cut.

He gave her that boyish, lopsided smile that had always made her tingle and feel guilty at the same time. She couldn't seem to make her mouth work.

"I almost didn't recognize you," he said. "You look different. Great though. Just, you know..." He shrugged, his dark blue eyes taking in her dress and legs. "Different."

She blinked to make sure he was real. She almost demanded to see the stupid, heart-shaped tattoo he'd gotten the night he and Gary had both scored low at the Laredo rodeo and blew their shot at the national finals. Drunk and reckless, they'd crossed into Mexico, looking for trouble. Hadn't taken them long to find it.

Kylie remembered well because she'd driven five hundred miles to bail them out. "What are you doing here?"

Landon gave his Stetson another twirl, then set it on his head and straightened away from the truck. "Is that it? Not even a hello?"

"There must be a rodeo in the area," she said, her brain scrambling to make sense of this—of Landon. Standing in front of her. How could he have gotten better looking in a year? And, whoa, that kind of thinking had to stop right now.

"No rodeo."

Of course not. She would've known. Even though she'd shied away from any talk related to the sport, anything new coming to the area had people buzzing for weeks. She didn't care how Gary was doing, whether good or bad. The knife of betrayal had cut too deep.

A horrifying thought occurred to her. She tried hard to peer through the tinted windows. "Is Gary with you?"

"Nope," Landon said, studying her closely. "Just me."

"I don't understand."

"I came to see you."

"Me? Why?"

"Look, Kylie," he said, sighing. "We…didn't exactly part on a good note, and that's bothered me. But I did as you asked and left you alone, even though it's not what I wanted."

Oh, God. The things she'd said to him her last night in Iowa. Any problems she'd had with Gary had nothing to do with Landon. At least not directly. If anything, her own guilt over having a thing for Landon had pushed her to blame him. The fuse had been lit the first day they'd met, and continued to spark, no matter how hard she fought it.

Landon had just returned to rodeo after taking a year off due to a family emergency. If she hadn't already been drawn to the way he smiled and those deep blue eyes, finding out he was a man who had his priorities straight would've sealed the deal for her.

She'd never acted on the attraction, even though it had gotten too close for comfort. Despite everything, she'd been certain it was going to be her and Gary forever. Even during those last two rough years when Gary had changed.

She'd done her best to treat Landon like everyone else. Even though he was nothing like the rest of Gary's friends. He'd always complimented her cooking, never once forgot to thank her, and always insisted on helping her clean the kitchen.

That small rented house had been open to Gary's friends. A lot of the guys had come and gone as they pleased. But Landon Kincaid had been the only one who'd kept her up at night with guilt.

"Kylie?"

She blinked. "What?"

Landon smiled. "We're still friends, aren't we?"

"I don't know." She felt a little dizzy. "Are we?"

"I wouldn't be standing here if I thought otherwise."

"How did you know I was here?"

"Your mom."

"My mom. Figures. Does Gary know?" she asked, holding her breath. All she needed was him showing up and causing a scene.

Landon's expression tightened. "If you're still hung up on him, Kylie, you need to tell me right now."

"Are you serious? Do I look like a doormat?" She bristled, then gave in to curiosity. "Why would you even care?"

His eyes narrowed, then flickered with amusement. "Oh, I don't know," he said quietly. "Maybe because we're friends."

She knew—they both did—that it was more than that. But a year had come and gone, and he still thought about her? She'd never stopped thinking about him, either, but that was different. Wasn't it?

She couldn't do a thing about the heat of embarrassment crawling up her neck and into her face. But she could stand her ground. "Friends or not," she said, "you didn't even give me the courtesy of a heads-up."

"True. I guess I was worried you'd—" Lifting a shoulder, he glanced away and dragged a hand down his unshaven jaw as he watched a truck cruise by. "Is that motel with the red roof the only one in town?"

"There's a small inn at the other end of Main Street." Kylie's heart fluttered. "How long are you staying?"

"A week, maybe two." He stared back, watching her closely enough it made her edgy. "If that's all right with you."

Jeez, it was hard to keep her expression neutral. To shove aside the curiosity, excitement and fear churning in her stomach. Normally she wasn't one to compare people, but the difference between her ex and Landon was glaringly obvious.

Gary had been strictly a rodeo junkie, but Landon was the real thing. The epitome of the strong silent cowboy depicted by Hollywood. Not only was he a born rancher, he was unfailingly polite and he always managed to hold on to his temper no matter how angry or disappointed he was. In fact, Landon seldom gave away his thoughts. He could be so stoic at times, unless he was trying to make a point.

But he also didn't make promises to women that he had no intention of keeping. Or at least that's what she wanted to believe.

She shouldn't have been angry with him. He hadn't encouraged Gary to start drinking and cheating. But he hadn't told Kylie about Gary two-timing her, either. And that hurt. Everyone following the tour must've known. Sure, he'd toed the line when she'd joined him at the nearby rodeos, but when she hadn't been in the stands, he'd indulged to his heart's content. All while she was back in Iowa being the good girl, keeping the home fires burning and waiting for her man.

Her useless, lying, cheating man.

Well, to hell with being the good girl. She wouldn't touch her neckline. It could plunge to her navel for all she cared.

"Last I spoke with Gary, he didn't know where you were," Landon said, breaking into her thoughts. "Is he still calling?"

Surprised that he wouldn't know what was going on with his best buddy, Kylie wasn't quick to reply. "He slowed down six months ago. I still get the occasional call but I haven't spoken to him. The times he left messages he sounded drunk."

Landon gave a slow, troubled nod. His gaze wandered down the front of her dress to her high heels—only three inches, but high for her. He lingered on her red-painted toenails, a ghost of a smile tugging at his mouth. "Did I tell you how nice you look?"

"Yes," she said. Great. Here her blush had just begun to settle. "Thank you."

"I don't recall ever seeing you in anything but T-shirts and jeans."

"They're comfortable and practical." She gestured to the bakery. "No point in dressing fancy. I'm always spilling something."

Landon chuckled. "I remember," he said, and looked into the bakery window and then at the sign. "You always said you'd open a bakery someday. And you did it. Good for you, Kylie. I'm proud of you."

Sincerity darkened his eyes and stirred something in her chest. "Save the sentiment until I start making a profit. I'm in debt up to my eyeballs."

"You can't have been open long. Wait till word spreads. You'll have people coming from miles away for your apple turnovers and chocolate dream cake."

"Oh, word is going to spread all right," she muttered when a truck nearly rear-ended a white compact because the driver was too busy gawking at her and Landon. It wasn't the first curious stare either.

Landon glanced down the street. "Ah, small-town living," he said. "You getting used to it yet?"

"Well, it's not like I came from the city. Sage Springs isn't that much bigger and just as bad for gossip." The words were no sooner out of her mouth when the memories rushed back. The pitying looks, the averted gazes, the whispers…

And not just in the neighborhood. She hadn't been able to put gas in her car or run into the market without someone mentioning they'd heard she and Gary had broken up. And wasn't it just awful, especially with them being *high school sweethearts* and all. The day Kylie decided she'd slug the next person who used the stupid term was the day she started packing her things.

Clearly it hadn't been enough that Gary had spent most of his time on the road and she'd moved across town. She had to get away from everything and everyone. Her mom included. Darlene couldn't understand why Kylie was unwilling to give Gary a second chance. And a third and fourth, had it come to that. Though not because her mom liked Gary all that much. Darlene had always been quick to overlook a man's flaws as long as he kept coming back.

Landon had moved closer without her noticing. "I guess I should've called first," he said and touched Kylie's hand. "I can see you're on your way out."

"What?" Once again she'd lost track of the conversation. And then it registered.

Kevin.

How could she have forgotten? He was likely to show up at any minute. Talk about awkward. She moved her hand so Landon was no longer touching her.

"So, is it a big date?" he asked casually. "Or a night out with the girls?"

She noticed how his gaze drifted briefly in the direction Rachel had headed. "You were right the first time."

"Ah." Surprise flickered in his eyes. Followed by disappointment if she wasn't mistaken. "Lousy timing on my part, huh?" he said, and moved back a couple steps.

"I'm not sure what that—" Kylie thought she noticed a limp. "Is something wrong with your leg?"

"Nah." Landon brushed her off too quickly.

"What happened?"

"Nothing. It's fine." He frowned at something behind her. "Is that him?"

She glanced back. Kevin, who'd just gotten out of his

red Mustang convertible, was wearing dress pants and a navy blue blazer and as nice and as good-looking as he was, he couldn't hold a candle to the cowboy she'd never expected to see again.

Chapter Three

"Guess you're stepping up in the world," Landon murmured low, so the dude with the crisp white shirt and shiny black shoes couldn't hear.

"What are you talking about?"

"Mr. *GQ*...isn't he your date?"

Kylie laughed, and it was the best sound he'd heard in a very long time. Then she ruined it by turning to smile at the interloper. Although, technically, it was Landon who'd shown up unannounced and uninvited.

"Kylie, you look stunning." The guy's gaze took in the low neckline, the way the red dress hugged the curve of her hips.

"Thank you." Blushing, she leaned over and kissed his cheek.

He seemed surprised, which made Landon feel a lot better. Couldn't be anything serious if that little peck raised the guy's eyebrows.

"Well, you kids have fun," Landon said, trying to ignore the pain that shot up his leg when he stepped back the wrong way.

"Wait. Let me introduce you two." Kylie's smile faltered when her date slipped an arm around her shoulders. "Landon, this is Kevin Braun." She turned to him, dislodging his arm. "This is Landon Kincaid, an old friend of mine."

Landon was forced to move forward. Grinding his teeth harder with each step, he shook the man's hand.

"You staying long, or just passing through?" Kevin asked. His tone was casual but Landon wasn't fooled.

"Staying," Landon said, and noticed how Kevin's jaw tightened. "Hey, I don't want to hold you guys up. I'll see you tomorrow, huh, Kylie?"

She frowned at his leg. "I can see you're hurting. Why won't you tell me what happened?"

"Tomorrow," Landon assured her, wishing they'd leave already so he could hobble and whimper in peace.

"Where are you staying?" Kevin asked.

"I'm gonna check out the motel."

Kevin pulled out his wallet. "I manage the place," he said, holding out a business card. "Give this to Patty at the front desk. She'll know to give you a discount. How long did you say you're staying?"

"Don't know for sure." Landon pocketed the card. "Thanks, Kevin. That's real nice of you."

"My pleasure." He turned to Kylie with a smile. "Ready?"

She was still studying Landon's leg, so he bit down hard and managed to walk around his truck without too obvious a limp.

Landon heard her say something to him, but pretended he hadn't and slid in behind the wheel. The sooner he checked in someplace where he could stretch out, the better. He thought briefly about having a look at the other inn that Kylie had mentioned. The motel seemed fine but he wasn't keen on Kevin keeping tabs on his comings and goings.

By the time he pulled away from the curb, the two

were on their way to Kevin's Mustang, his hand pressed against Kylie's lower back.

Landon reminded himself that he hadn't been at all sure how she'd react to seeing him. She'd been living here for a year. Plenty of time to carve out a nice life for herself. Hell, it wasn't a surprise that some guy had swooped in—there'd probably been quite a few.

Part of him was glad because after what Gary had done to her, Kylie deserved to feel desirable and wanted. The other part of him itched to send Kevin on a one-way trip to the moon. Though Landon didn't think she was too into the guy. He knew Kylie pretty well, probably better than she suspected.

Or did he?

He turned into the motel parking lot, wondering what she was doing with a buttoned-up guy like Kevin. This rural corner of Montana had to be crawling with ranchers and hired hands. Had she sworn off cowboys like she'd said that night? Decided they were all lying cheats like Gary? Landon figured he'd find out real soon.

THE NEXT MORNING, her arms loaded with bakery boxes, Kylie looked for Landon's truck as she crossed the motel parking lot. There it was, the deep maroon color easy to spot. He'd parked in the far corner, away from all the other vehicles. Probably worried about his paint job. Not that she blamed him. The truck looked new. She wondered how he'd scraped the money together to replace his old white pickup with the duct-taped side mirrors.

She'd come extra early to deliver the motel's standing order of muffins and Danish for their continental breakfast. From what she remembered, Landon wasn't a particularly early riser but she decided not to take any chances. Of course she couldn't avoid him for long, but she was too tired to see him first thing.

Once she opened the bakery, she'd have a steady stream of customers. So even if he showed up right away, she'd be too busy to talk.

Patty, who worked the front desk, was setting out plates and utensils when Kylie entered the lobby. The strong smell of coffee had her inhaling deeply, as if she hadn't already downed half a pot.

"Hey," Patty said, looking over at her. "I figured you'd be late, not twenty minutes early."

"Why would you—" Kylie sighed and set down the boxes. No telling how many people knew she'd gone out with Kevin last night. Any news was big news in this town. "What are you doing here? Didn't you work late yesterday?"

"I swapped shifts with Misty so I can go to my son's ball game this evening." Patty gave her a little teasing smile. "Did you have fun last night?"

"We had dinner at an Italian restaurant in Kalispell. It was nice."

"And?"

"And what? We didn't stay out late. I had to get up early to do the baking. Which reminds me…you mentioned you have a friend who's looking for part-time work?"

Patty nodded. "Celeste. She was hoping you needed kitchen help. She likes to work early shifts so she can be home for her kids after school. Plus, she's a great baker."

"Perfect. I'll get her number from you or she can call me." Kylie was happy they'd changed the subject, and even happier that she might get someone to take some of the pressure off her in the mornings. She'd never imagined a town the size of Blackfoot Falls would keep her so busy.

"Go grab some coffee in the back," Patty said as she set out the muffins on doily-covered silver trays.

"Thanks, but I've got to get back and open." She glanced toward the elevator. "What time do the guests start coming down?"

"There's always one or two who show up at the stroke of seven." She checked her watch. "We've got twenty minutes. You sure you don't want a cup? I broke out the good stuff."

Kylie laughed. Patty couldn't be more obvious. She wanted the skinny on Kylie's date with her boss. But there was nothing to tell. Kylie had been distracted most of the evening. It wasn't fair to Kevin. He'd been wonderful and thoughtful, and she'd tried her best to return the attention. But she hadn't been able to stop thinking of Landon.

What made things worse was that Kevin was exactly the kind of man she should be looking for. He was the sort of steady, reliable man she wanted in her life. Not someone who would live for the adrenaline of bucking broncos and didn't mind living out of a duffel bag. She wished, though, that he was a little more exciting. But excitement wasn't all it was cracked up to be. Kylie had finally accepted his third dinner invitation. And she planned to accept another date…soon-ish.

She sniffed the air. Macadamia Kona roast. Darn it.

"Come on," Patty said. "Just one cup. Five minutes. Before Marge brings her cinnamon rolls."

"You're evil."

Patty grinned. "Let me cover these trays and I'll meet you in the back."

The room behind the front desk was small and crowded with a full-size fridge, a microwave, two large coffee stations and overstocked shelves. She followed the aroma of the Kona coffee to the small carafe sitting off to the side. Kylie had just poured herself a mug when she heard Marge's voice. Marge owned the diner and her cinnamon rolls—a local favorite—were insanely good.

Kylie liked her. Marge had been supportive of her opening The Cake Whisperer, even giving her tips on where to get her supplies and ingredients. And best of all, she'd probably just saved Kylie from being cross-examined.

After adding a dollop of cream, Kylie stirred her coffee and yawned so wide she felt her jaw pop. Kevin had dropped her off by ten, but she hadn't slept well. Too much Landon on the brain. Boy, the next few days were going to be tricky. Or for however long he stuck around. That limp she'd noticed... Was that the reason he wasn't rushing off to a rodeo? Did he think good ole Kylie would play nursemaid, the way she had in the past? She'd been known to treat and bandage minor wounds for a lot of Gary's friends. Landon included.

Evidently the two women hadn't missed her. They were chatting and laughing as if they didn't see each other every morning. Kylie paused at the slightly open door to take a leisurely sip.

And nearly burned her tongue when she heard Landon's voice.

She gave the door a slight push. Just wide enough that she could see him, but he couldn't see her. He was fishing an apple out of the silver bowl sitting next to the muffins. Neither Marge or Patty noticed her because they were too busy checking out Landon. He filled out a pair of worn jeans better than any man Kylie had ever met. The snug white T-shirt showed just how seriously he took his workouts. Though it wasn't vanity that drove him to keep fit. He loved rodeoing and took the sport seriously.

"Hope you slept well," Patty said. "We've been open less than a year so the mattresses are all new."

Landon flashed her a smile. "It was lights out before I hit the pillow." He eyed the plastic-wrapped trays. "Guess I'm too early. I'll let you finish setting up and come back."

"Don't be silly." Patty gestured to a club chair. "You go on and sit down. I'll get your coffee and whatever else you need."

"Nah. I'm good for now. But thanks." He grabbed a crutch that was resting against the wall and slipped it under his arm.

Kylie hadn't noticed it because his body had blocked her view. When he swung toward her she saw the second crutch. Their eyes met through the doorway and he lost his footing. He quickly righted himself by balancing on one leg until he stabilized the crutches.

"What are you doing here?" he asked as she moved out into the lobby.

"What happened to your leg?"

"Nothing."

"Oh, okay. I guess crutches are the new fashion trend."

"That's right." His hair hadn't been combed and stubble darkened his chin and jaw.

"Shut up," Kylie said, annoyed at the flutter in her chest. "Tell me what happened."

"I broke my leg. No big deal."

"It is if *you're* using crutches." She studied the leg he was favoring. "You're not wearing a cast."

"Yeah, it came off a few days ago."

"By you or the doctor?"

Landon's sigh sounded like guilt.

Kylie gaped at him. "Seriously?"

"The doctor was being overly cautious. She wanted to leave it on a week longer and I convinced her I was ready."

"Yeah, I bet."

Patty smothered a laugh. Marge just cut loose a howl that probably woke the other guests.

How could Kylie have forgotten they had an audience? She glanced over at them. "We're old friends."

"Ah." Patty's grin widened.

"Did you bring me coffee?" Landon asked, staring at the steaming mug warming her palms.

"Oh, right, I ran over to make sure it was all ready for you the second you came down." Kylie had no problem wiping the hopeful expression from his face now that she'd confirmed her suspicion. Wasn't he going to be shocked when she told him she was done playing nursemaid?

But first she had to quit worrying about his stupid leg. *Convincing* his doctor to take off the cast early…what an idiot. Landon was smarter than that.

He stood balanced on his crutches, taking in the loaded trays. "Ah. You brought the pastries," he said, a self-deprecating smile curving his mouth. "Okay. My bad." He glanced at the two women avidly watching them, and gave them a polite nod. "I'll see you all later."

Before he could swing around on his crutches, Kylie let out a huff and said, "For heaven's sake, sit down."

"Nope. Don't want to be a bother." He kept moving toward the elevator without so much as a backward glance. "Thanks for the apple."

"Landon."

The elevator door opened as soon as he pushed the

button, as if it had been waiting for him, and he took the last few steps rather quickly.

Kylie couldn't see his face as the door slid closed, which was just as well. She wasn't at all pleased with the soft gooey feeling in her chest. Landon was a big boy, he could fend for himself. His family had a ranch in Wyoming. He should've gone there to recuperate.

"Good Lord, girl."

She turned to Patty. "What?"

"What?" Both women laughed. Patty, who was in her early forties and happily married, said, "Very nice."

"Why on earth would you chase him away?" Still chuckling, Marge shook her graying head. "I thought you had a date with Kevin last night."

"Landon's just an old friend."

"Uh-huh," they said in unison, staring at her, curiosity mirrored in both pairs of eyes.

Oh, this wasn't going to work. Kylie took a final sip of the cooling coffee. "Thanks for this," she told Patty.

"Wait. Where are you going?"

She slipped into the back room and poured out the rest of her mug and rinsed it. "I have to go get ready to open."

"Yeah, but you still have—"

She didn't let Patty finish. Kylie hurried through the small lobby and out the door. Which was the completely wrong move because now she'd just complicated the situation. Made it look much worse than it was. She hadn't lied. They were only friends. Or used to be.

Dammit.

Chapter Four

Landon sat in his truck outside the bakery waiting for the morning rush to ease. Not that anyone seemed to be in any hurry. Eleven minutes was the average time it took a customer to place their order, pay for it and bend Kylie's ear. He'd kept track out of sheer boredom.

When an elderly woman stopped to peer in through the window, he decided that was it. He could be waiting forever. The small Wyoming town where he'd grown up hadn't been any different. Some of the older folks were likely to pass the morning talking about nothing. And Kylie, softhearted as she was, would worry they were lonely and let them monopolize her time.

He got out of the truck, dragging the crutches out with him. It wasn't as if Kylie didn't know about his injury. And damn, he couldn't afford to be careless.

After some clumsy maneuvering, he opened the door and managed to cross the threshold without falling on his ass. When he glanced up he met Kylie's gaze. She was standing behind the counter wearing a pink apron over her T-shirt and jeans and her hair was pulled back into a ponytail.

Wariness flickered in her hazel eyes before she re-focused on the customer asking about a birthday cake for her grandson. Three other women were chatting as they waited their turn.

The space was smaller than he'd thought, with wood laminate floors, pale yellow walls and white clouds painted on the light blue ceiling. But no place to sit. So he settled in the corner where he wouldn't be in the way, and leaned on his crutches as he waited.

The smell of fresh-brewed coffee drifted over to him. He didn't see a coffeepot, and couldn't tell if the aroma was coming from the kitchen or from the counter behind Kylie.

"Yoo-hoo, young man?"

Landon turned to the tiny, white-haired woman trying to get his attention. She waved him over to where she stood near the case. He sighed. Why had he thought the crutches would give him a pass?

He hobbled over to her. "Yes, ma'am, how can I help?" he asked with a polite smile.

"You can park yourself right here," she said, gesturing to the spot in front of her. "Kylie can take your order next. No need for you to be waiting, you being a cripple and all."

Cripple.

Landon tried not to cringe. "Well, that's very kind of you," he said, "but I'm just waiting for Kylie."

"Oh, you're a friend of hers?" she asked, curiosity etched in every line on her face.

The other women all turned and checked him out.

"I have a chair in the back," Kylie said quickly. "Why don't you wait there? I'll even bring you a cup of coffee."

"Can't pass up that offer," he said and nodded at the elderly woman, who looked disappointed. "You have a real nice day, ma'am."

The place was utterly quiet as everyone watched him

hobble around the counter, which made him feel awkward as hell.

"It's just a folding chair," Kylie said as he was about to enter the kitchen. "I'll bring your coffee in a minute."

"I can get it myself." He spotted the coffee station directly behind her on the back counter. "Take care of your customers. I'm good."

"Oh, don't you worry about us," said the tall woman ordering the birthday cake. "We have all the time in the world."

The other three nodded.

Yeah, just what he wanted to hear.

"Well, I'm afraid I don't," Kylie said, turning to a pair of solid-looking upper oak cabinets and bringing down a three-ring binder. "Tell you what, Shirley, why don't you have a look at these pictures of other cakes I've done while I box Eunice's turnovers?"

Landon saw the mugs stacked in the open cabinet and leaned his crutches against the wall.

"What do you mean you don't have time, dear? Will you be closing early?"

"Oh, for pity's sake, Mabel. She has plans with the hunk."

Slanting the eighty-something woman a quick look, Landon realized she meant him.

Kylie laughed. "Actually, I have Joe Hopkins coming at eleven-thirty."

"What for?" Shirley had stepped aside as she flipped through the pages.

"To give me a quote on raising part of this front counter to accommodate some bar stools."

"Bar stools?" Mabel repeated, frowning. "How do you expect us to climb up on those?"

Just as Landon squeezed in behind Kylie, he noticed

that the rosy-cheeked Mabel and the woman standing beside her were twins. And that Kylie had stiffened up the way she used to when Gary said something stupid.

"Actually, the counter isn't so much about a place to sit," Kylie said. "I'll be setting up a coffee station on the other end—"

"You mean you're going to start serving all those expensive coffees I see on the TV commercials?" Mabel looked at her sister, who'd scrunched up her face as if she'd swallowed something sour.

"Just a couple of specialty flavors, but nothing else will change. I promise."

"Why can't you bring in a table and some chairs for us older folks?"

"It's really too small in here," Kylie said, keeping her voice conciliatory. "But I'm hoping to expand and then—"

"These cakes are something else," Shirley cut in. "Would you mind if I borrowed this to show my daughter-in-law?"

"Not at all," Kylie said eagerly. "In fact, I have—" She turned and slammed right into him.

The side of his head smacked the cabinet door.

Her eyes widened. A gasp slipped past her lips as he caught her waist to steady himself.

"Oh, I'm so sorry." She touched his face, her slender fingers as gentle as butterfly wings. "Are you okay?"

"Fine."

She swept the hair off his forehead. "It's red. You'll have a lump."

Her sweet breath tempted him to move closer. To taste those lush pink lips he'd been dreaming about for years. "Nah. You always said I was hardheaded."

"True." She lowered her hand. And jerked back. "Your leg...did I—"

"My leg is fine, Kylie." He wondered if she remembered they were being watched. He looked in the cabinet and brought down a stack of flattened white cardboard. "Will this size work for the turnovers?"

She blinked at the cardboard, then looked back at him. "Why are you here, Landon?"

"Let's save that discussion for later, huh?" The last thing he wanted to do was embarrass her, but he was pretty sure she'd spaced. Keeping his gaze locked with hers, he started assembling boxes. "Your customer's waiting for her turnovers."

"Good heavens, don't fret over me."

Comprehension widened Kylie's eyes. After a quick glance at their eager audience, she grabbed a box out of his hands. "Eunice, I have your favorites this morning," she said, reaching into the glass case with a pair of silver tongs. "One apple and two cherry, right?"

"Well, no, actually I—"

Before the woman finished speaking, Kylie taped the box shut. "Here you go. I'm sorry for the wait."

Looking puzzled, Eunice just nodded and laid some money on the counter.

Mabel whispered something to her sister and they both giggled like teenagers.

Shirley had closed the binder and was staring over her glasses at Landon. She was quite a bit younger than the other three, maybe in her midfifties. And tall enough that she nearly came eye-to-eye with him.

A timer beeped in the kitchen. Kylie mumbled something about checking the oven and hurried into the back.

Landon brought down a mug and poured himself some

coffee. Forgetting where he'd left the crutches, he glanced around and discovered he was still in Shirley's crosshairs.

He took a sip, then smiled at her. "Go ahead," he said. "I know you've got something to say. Let's hear it."

She tucked the binder under her arm. "Kylie's a sweet girl. She might not have lived here long, but she's like one of our own." Her eyes narrowed. "You got that, cowboy?"

"Yes, ma'am, I do."

"Now, what did you do to your leg?"

"Got bucked off a horse."

"Rodeo?"

Landon nodded.

"You ride professionally?"

Again he nodded, and reached for his crutches. This wasn't a conversation he wanted to have. By now he was fairly certain Kylie hadn't been following rodeo news and had no idea how high he was ranked. And that suited him fine.

"I thought you looked familiar."

"My word, I thought so, too," Mabel said, leaning closer and squinting at him.

Her sister huffed with annoyance. "You did no such thing," she said, clutching her white sack. "If you want a ride home you'd better be right behind me."

The pair bickered all the way out the door. Through the window Landon watched them stop at a big Chevy that had to be over twenty years old. "Should they be driving?"

"No." Shirley chuckled. "But they don't go far and everyone knows to give them a wide berth." She glanced at her watch. "I need to get going too. Eunice, would you like a ride home?"

"Well…" The elderly woman peered toward the kitchen and then looked back at Landon.

"I'm meeting my daughter in Kalispell," Shirley said. "It's now or never."

Eunice nodded. "It was nice to meet you, young man."

"Likewise."

"Remember what I told you," Shirley said, wagging a finger as they headed for the door.

"Yes, ma'am." He caught her little grin as she turned her head and figured he'd passed inspection.

They'd barely made it outside when a woman, who looked too young to have a toddler resting on her hip, paused at the window.

He cursed under his breath. Maybe if he hung the Closed sign for a—

"Sorry about that. I had to pull out the cupcakes—" Kylie stopped in the doorway. "What did you do, chase away all my customers?"

"I wish." He glanced toward the window.

She followed his gaze and grinned. "Oh, that's Mary Sara," she said, waving. "She won't come in until after she goes to the bank."

"Don't you have any help?"

"I did. There was a teenager who used to come in after school, but she left for college last month. I'm pretty sure I'll have someone else starting soon." Kylie blew at the stray wisps of hair fluttering around her face. Her cheeks were flushed, probably from the heat of the oven.

Though he'd like to think he had a little something to do with it.

The way she watched him sip his coffee sent his heart rate into overdrive. When he realized she wanted to smooth her hair back without using her hands, he reached over to help her out.

She ducked. "Why don't you come on back with me

while I make some frosting," she said, pulling her gaze away. "At least you can sit."

Without waiting for a response, she whirled around and retraced her steps.

Landon hung on to his mug and used one crutch to follow her. "So, you might be able to expand?"

"That depends on a number of things." Kylie sighed. "I can't believe I brought up the bar stools. That was so dumb. I wanted to play down the whole city coffee bar thing."

"Better they know ahead of time, right? So they get used to the idea."

"I can't afford to alienate my customers, and honestly I don't want to hurt their feelings. Most of them are just nice, lonely old women."

"So, then what about two small tables?"

"In that little corner? I'm busy in the morning and the tables would just be in the way."

"I meant really small, like those round tables you see in cocktail lounges. That should fit."

"With chairs, too?" She shook her head. "Anyway, I'm trying to preserve the rustic feel of the place to balance out the coffee bar. Keep it from looking like I've gotten too citified."

"Okay. I get it," he said. "How about a couple of bench seats built against the wall? That wouldn't take up much space. Make 'em right, and people won't be camping out all day."

Kylie laughed. "Are you saying the seats shouldn't be too comfortable?"

He just grinned.

The kitchen was old but spotless, which wasn't surprising. In between rodeos some of Gary's so-called *friends* had used the house he and Kylie shared as a crash pad.

Yet Kylie had always managed to keep the place clean. Landon had mentioned something about it not being fair to her, and Gary had blown up at him. Told him it was none of his goddamn business. Landon couldn't argue with that.

Kylie stopped at a scarred butcher-block island that sat in the middle of the kitchen. Leaning against it was the metal folding chair. "This is sturdier than it looks," she said, glancing at him as she set it up. "I should've brought your coffee. I'm sorry. Where's your other crutch?"

"I get along just fine with one." Closing in on the island, he took the last foot with a short hop on his good leg. Coffee sloshed over the rim onto his hand.

"Uh-huh." A grin teased the corners of her lips. "You were saying?"

"No fair. You're making me nervous."

"Me?" She let out a laugh. "Please."

"Come here."

Wariness changed her expression. "Why?"

"Jesus, I'm not gonna bite."

She slowly rounded the island. The second she was within reach, he caught her wrist and held her hand against his chest. "You feel how fast my heart's beating?"

"So what? So is mine." Her eyes widened when she realized what she'd just admitted. The second she tugged her hand back he let her go.

While he still had his wits about him, he said, "I figure we can call it even."

Her cheeks matched her pink apron and made her eyes sparkle like emeralds. He wanted to kiss her so bad, but he might have waited too long to reenter her life. He owed it to her to wait and see where she stood.

Chapter Five

Kylie combined the ingredients for the frosting in a bowl while Landon got comfortable. The darn man had been in town only a matter of hours and already he was making her jittery.

"Tell me about the expansion. What does it depend on?"

"Well, the city owns the building and they use the space next door for town meetings. Sadie—she's the mayor—thinks they should move to a bigger location. If they do, she'll give me first crack at renting it."

"How big is the place?"

"Big," she said as she got busy whipping in the chocolate. "I wouldn't have to rent the whole thing. They could break it down. I'd still have plenty of room for tables and chairs, and I could build up the coffee bar business, too."

He was quiet for such a long time that she glanced up at him. Oddly, he was staring at the mixing bowl and frowning.

"What's wrong?"

"Hmm?" He met her eyes. "Nothing. When do you see something like that happening?"

"Maybe never. I just don't know at this point. Anyway, it wouldn't be cheap since I'd have to knock down part of the wall. I'd have to save up."

"So, you're getting a quote just on the counter?"

She nodded. "And a matching condiment cabinet."

"Sounds like a good place to start."

"Except for the older customers." She started icing the cupcakes for the special order that would be picked up soon. Hyperaware of Landon watching her, Kylie fumbled the spatula and gouged a hole in the third cupcake. Calmly, she set down the spatula before she did something stupid, like throw it against the wall.

"Did you do that on purpose?"

She looked up and saw that he wasn't joking. "Why on earth would I do that?"

"I don't know." He shrugged. "Maybe to put something extra in it?"

"Like what?"

Ignoring her snippy tone, he asked, "What is it they put in those cakes during Mardi Gras in New Orleans?"

Kylie managed to shake her head without rolling her eyes. He was just trying to help. No reason to snap at him.

"Okay, look," he said. "Why don't you give me something to do? No sense me just sitting here."

"I agree. Why don't you go have some lunch at the diner? Or go relax in your room?"

"Trying to get rid of me, Kylie?" He spoke evenly, without a trace of accusation or annoyance or anything at all. Idling in neutral was typical for Landon.

"After all that driving I figured your leg must be stiff and you might want to stretch it." She went to the sink and washed her hands. Mostly to avoid his probing eyes. "By the way, how was the motel?"

"Not bad. The bed was comfortable. Kevin's business card got me a good discount," Landon said. "How was your date?"

Thank God she had her back to him. Even knowing

the question was inevitable hadn't helped her prepare. And just because she wasn't facing him didn't mean he'd stopped staring. So hard she could almost feel her skin burn. "It was nice."

His prolonged silence finally got to her.

Hoping and praying the bell over the door would ring, she grabbed a dish towel. Not a single customer for almost thirty minutes. Now, they all stayed away? As she turned to face him, she concentrated on drying her hands. "Tell me about your leg."

A smile curved his mouth and struck a raw nerve. "Are you going out with him again?"

Kylie felt her blood pressure climb. "How is that any of your business?"

He shrugged. "I'd just hate to see you get mixed up with a guy who isn't right for you just to *show* me."

"Show you *what*? I hadn't given you a second thought until yesterday."

After studying her for a few seconds, he said, "I thought about you a lot."

She could barely catch her breath. "I don't blame you for Gary's behavior. You can stop feeling—"

"It had nothing to do with Gary." One side of his mouth hiked up. Not in a smile exactly. More like a challenge as his gaze held hers steady. "At least not in the way you're thinking."

Kylie swallowed. The look he was giving her scrambled her brain. She'd seen it before, over the years when she'd caught him watching her. She never understood how she could panic and melt at the same time. As it was, she'd almost done something unforgivable.

"Who's been taking care of you?" she asked, darting a look at his leg.

"First, I take care of myself just fine. Second, I didn't

come all this way for you to be my nurse. Or to discuss Gary. Or to rehash the past."

"Okay." She cleared her throat. "Then I'll ask you again, why are you here?"

"That answer hasn't changed since yesterday. But I've got a question for you," he said, and there it was again. Although it seemed to be more an entreaty than a challenge this time.

The bell over the door rang.

Thank God.

"Excuse me. I have a customer," she murmured and hurried up front.

Mallory was holding the door open and looking back at the street. She turned when she saw Kylie. "Hey, how did it go last night?"

"Good. Great, really." Kylie tilted her head to see who Mallory was holding the door for.

"Rachel was right behind me." Mallory let go of the door. "I should've known she'd get sidetracked."

"Nope. I'm here." Rachel caught the door before it closed and rushed inside, her eyes bright and eager. "So, tell us everything."

Mallory gave Kylie a sympathetic smile. "Where did you guys go?"

"Dinner in Kalispell."

"Your hair looks terrific, by the way," Mallory said. "I love those highlights."

"I like it, too," Kylie murmured, moving to the end of the counter where there was less chance of Landon overhearing.

Rachel frowned. "Where are you going?"

Kylie had to think fast. If it was only Mallory she could've given her a nonverbal sign. But not Rachel. "I'm thinking of making this area more like a coffee bar. What do you think?"

"You already told us that," Rachel said. "I'm more interested in your date with Kevin."

"I told you, we went to dinner."

"Oh, honey, I don't care about that." Rachel sighed. "I want to know if you got laid."

Suddenly her friends both jerked a look toward the kitchen, and Kylie knew… Darn him, why couldn't he have stayed put?

Landon stood in the doorway, his mug in hand. "I was kinda wondering that myself," he said and winked at Kylie. He smiled at the other two. "I'm Landon. But don't mind me, I'm just getting more coffee."

Rachel stared, her mouth slightly open.

Mallory chuckled. "I don't believe it. Rachel is speechless."

"Oh, my God," Rachel said, with a quick glance at Kylie. "You have so much to tell us."

"Thanks, Mallory. You couldn't leave well enough alone?" Kylie saw that Landon had drained the coffee and was about to make another pot. "Go," she said, taking the filters from him and pointing to the kitchen. "I'll take care of this."

"Oh, no." Rachel pressed a hand to her tummy. "The smell will kill me."

"Then you'd better leave," Kylie said, already measuring the grounds.

"That's so mean."

"I'll talk to you later."

"Come on, Rach." Mallory took her arm and steered her toward the door.

"I'm Rachel Gunderson," she called to Landon. "I look forward to visiting with you."

He stopped and turned. "Any relation to Matt Gunderson?"

"Who do you think knocked me up?" Rubbing her stomach, she sighed as Mallory dragged her outside.

"Matt's wife?" Landon asked once the door closed.

Kylie nodded. "They have a ranch south of here. Do you know him?"

"I've met him. I used to see him around before he left the tour. I'd forgotten he was from around here." He glanced out the window. "Matt's a champion bull rider. He was at the top of his game when he just up and quit. He shocked everybody."

"Oh, you mean because there really is life after rodeo?" She immediately regretted her sarcasm but there was nothing to do about it now.

Landon shook his head. "It's not unheard of. What's he doing these days? Raising cattle?"

"Primarily. The Lone Wolf has been in his family for generations, but I think his focus is on raising rodeo stock. He's already produced two champion bulls."

"So you are keeping up with rodeo news?"

"No. They're my friends. I keep up with *them*." Kylie poured in the water, grateful she had a reason to avoid Landon's gaze.

He wasn't so quick to fill the silence. He leaned against the counter, watching her. "What's going on here, Kylie?"

"Nothing."

"I understand why you're hurt and angry with Gary but—"

"*Was* hurt and angry. Past tense. I rarely think about him anymore." She saw doubt in his eyes and shrugged. "Believe what you want but that's the truth. I'm happy here. I have friends. Real friends." She noticed his slight cringe. She hadn't meant it as a jab.

"Are you staying with your aunt?"

"I did for the first couple months. Then Mallory, the woman with Rachel, moved, and I took over the house she'd been renting. It's small, just two bedrooms, but it has a big porch, a nice backyard, and it's right off Main Street."

"Sounds perfect for you."

"It is." She noticed he'd shifted his weight. "Let's go back to the kitchen so you can sit down."

Without arguing, he turned around. "Mind grabbing that crutch for me?"

It was the one he'd left behind so he could carry his mug. Instead of waiting for her to pass it to him, he limped into the kitchen ahead of her.

Kylie shot a glance out the window to make sure no customers were about to come in before she followed him. "Something's wrong with this picture."

He looked at the crutch she held up. "I don't need it. I just didn't want it in your way." He sure looked relieved when he sank onto the chair, though.

"So what, it's just for decoration?"

"I meant I didn't need it for this short a distance."

"Ah." She leaned the crutch on the island where he could reach it.

"Hey, I've been doing everything the physical therapist instructed me to do. You think I wanna stay benched? Every rodeo I sit out costs me money and a chance at the finals."

Kylie darted him a look but he'd shut down. His expression went blank. "You must be ranked high to be thinking about the finals."

He shrugged. "I was doing pretty well until this happened." He gestured to the injured leg and practically snarled. "Talk about lousy timing."

"I can't imagine there's ever a good time for a broken leg," she said, and went to the sink and washed her hands. "I, on the other hand, do have a timing issue. I need to have this order ready by twelve-thirty."

Landon looked at the old clock on the wall beside the pantry and smiled. The picture of a fancy cupcake was captioned with *I Bake* in big bold letters, followed by *so I don't strangle people* in a dainty cursive used to hang in her kitchen. "You still have that."

"I tried getting rid of it but somehow it just wouldn't stay in the donation box." Her laugh ended in a sigh at the sight of the mangled cupcake. "Too bad you don't like chocolate cupcakes."

"Who says I don't?"

"Are you kidding? I must have made thousands of cupcakes over the years, and I don't think you touched a single one of them."

"Only because I knew you were filling orders. I didn't want to screw up your count."

She hadn't yet iced the six extra she'd made for the display case, so she snitched one from under the dish towel, then turned to Landon. "Well, you were the only one." She should've known, she thought. Landon had always been considerate like that. And Gary, who should've been supportive of her fledgling home business, well, he'd been just as bad as the rest of his thoughtless buddies.

At times he'd treated her like his personal maid, minus a paycheck. And what had Kylie done about it? Nothing. She'd made excuses for him, to herself, to her friends, to her mom...although that was easy. Her mother never had a problem giving a man a pass.

Thinking back to those horrible days shamed Kylie to her core. She couldn't bear to imagine what Landon had thought of her lack of backbone. And then to make things worse, she had a sudden flashback to that day she and Landon had almost kissed.

At the memory, her cheeks flamed. Why did her brain have to dig all that up now? This was exactly why Kevin was the right kind of man for her. She'd always know where he stood, and that job emergencies notwithstanding, when he'd be home each night.

"Kylie?" Landon's tone suggested this wasn't the first time he'd tried to get her attention.

Finally she looked at him, but it wasn't easy.

"What are you gonna do with that?" he asked, nodding at the ruined cupcake. "I'd be happy to take it off your hands."

"I thought you watched what you ate."

"Yeah, well, I'm allowed to cheat now and then. Especially when something smells this good."

Kylie heard the jingle of the bell over the door and handed Landon the cupcake. "I'll be right out," she called as she took off her apron.

"Take your time," Joe Hopkins replied in a gravelly voice.

"Stay here while I talk to Joe."

Landon put his hands up. "Whatever you say."

She didn't believe that for a minute.

Chapter Six

True to his word, Landon stayed in the kitchen. Though he didn't understand why she wanted him to hang back. Maybe she thought he'd butt in, which he wouldn't have done since he knew very little about carpentry.

He liked the other possibility better...that he was too big a distraction. Fair was fair. Thinking about her had given him a broken leg.

In the long run it didn't matter that he'd stayed in the kitchen. He could hear every bit of the conversation thanks to Joe's loud voice. The counter and cabinet didn't seem to be very complicated, and Landon was pleased that she asked about his idea for the bench seats. But after Joe quoted her a price for the whole job, Kylie was quick to ask him to give her a separate number for just the counter and cabinet. It took the guy a few minutes to revise his price, but even then, Kylie didn't commit to anything.

The fact that she wanted to keep the same rustic feel as most of the shops in town, but still give it an urban twist made it impossible for Landon to judge whether either quote was reasonable or not. All he knew for sure was that it had given Kylie pause.

Leaning his shoulder against the doorframe, he checked out the stout, middle-aged man as Kylie walked him to the door. Joe eyed him back and Landon gave him a friendly nod.

As soon as the man was gone, Landon stepped out of the kitchen. "You think he's charging too much?"

Kylie glanced at him, her brow furrowed in thought. "I honestly don't know," she said, then turned back to studying the wall as he moved over next to her. "You know," she said, without looking at him, "the bench seats really are a good idea."

"Joe seemed to think so, too."

"Yeah," she said, angling her hands in front of her as if she were visualizing the booths. "They'll still have to wait. I won't know for a while if this coffee bar idea will even work."

"What if you didn't have to pay for anything but the material?"

She looked at him as if he'd lost his mind. "I have my hands pretty full ruining cupcakes."

"I've got nothing but time for the next couple of weeks. I could probably handle it."

Her brow furrowed again. "With a busted leg."

"I'm not completely helpless. And there's got to be a local kid who could use a few bucks for helping me with the lifting. Right?"

"I think what you're supposed to be doing is recuperating."

"Right, but I still have to keep myself busy enough that I won't go insane. Seriously, Kylie, it can't be all that difficult." He hoped.

"What do you know about carpentry, anyway?"

"I grew up on a ranch. You think I didn't have to do my share of repairs?"

"That's not the same as building something from scratch."

She had a point there, but when she folded her arms across her chest, he couldn't seem to make heads or tails of what that point was.

But he didn't let his gaze linger. He needed to get a tight grip on his control or he was going to blow his best shot at getting close enough to Kylie to see if they could have something.

She studied him for a long time, but before she could speak, a couple of women walked in and while they clearly knew Kylie, they seemed to be a lot more interested in looking him over.

He needed to make himself scarce. It was easy to slip back into the kitchen and listen to the women chatting up a storm, while using the opportunity to call his brother. Chad was the handy one in the family.

"Hey, you got a minute?"

Chad snorted. "Yeah, I'm fine. And you?"

"Listen, I don't have much time. You can give me shit later." Landon kept one eye on Kylie while he described the work she wanted done, and named the price Joe had given her before Landon mentioned the tables and bench seats. "What do you think? That sound about right?"

"Hell, I can't answer that. I'd have to see the place. Why not buy tables and chairs? It'd be cheaper and faster."

"The place is small and kind of rustic. Bringing in furniture won't fit with her plans. Which is why I thought of setting up a couple of bench seats against the wall, with two small tables in front, and a chair or two."

"Good thinking. But that wasn't part of the quote."

"Yeah, I know. She wants the counter done first. Mostly I want to make sure the guy isn't ripping her off. It'll probably end up that he just builds the counter. As for the rest...you know, since I have some downtime..."

"Wait, wait. What are you saying?"

"I figured I'd take a stab at the benches and tables."

Chad's laugh didn't make Landon feel any better, but there was no time to argue. Kylie was boxing up some cupcakes. "Come on. Help me out here. There's gotta be a way I can pull this off."

"What kind of wood?"

"She mentioned oak, so I guess I'd go with that."

Chad hesitated. "Dude, really? You're thinking of doing this yourself?"

Landon had no idea what he was thinking. Although what he was considering didn't seem too complicated. All he cared about was not seeing Kylie disappointed.

"Who did you say this is for?"

"Okay, gotta change the subject," Landon said when he saw Kylie ring up the order. Chad grunted, prompting Landon to add, "No joke."

"Ah, this woman isn't just a friend."

When he didn't answer, Chad started laughing. Landon met Kylie's eyes and stepped back so she could enter the kitchen. "Mom isn't back yet, huh?"

"Nope. The end of next week."

"I'll come for a few days once she's settled."

"Figures. We've been haying. Could've used your help now."

"With a broken leg?"

Chad barked out a laugh. "You're looking for sympathy from *me*?"

"Good point," Landon said, glad they could finally laugh like this. After his brother's accident, there hadn't been much to laugh about for a long time.

"Anyway, hotshot, you could've run the baler. Just like I do," Chad said. "Hey, I've been meaning to ask, you're not still sending checks, are you?"

Damn. Landon had hoped the topic would never come up. "I've been laid up. I don't have money coming in." It wasn't a lie, even if it didn't really answer the question.

"If you're sending some to Mom so she can go on her trips, that's something else. But the ranch is doing fine. In fact, we made more money this past year than we have since we lost Dad."

"Huh." Apparently his mom hadn't been stretching the truth. "Glad to hear it."

"You don't sound like it."

"What? No, I am. I just got distracted. Sorry."

"I figured you might be pouting because Martin and I are doing so well without you."

"Screw you." Landon forced a laugh. His brother had struck him where it hurt. He'd also confirmed a suspicion Landon had been harboring for the past six months. Good thing he'd planted the seed that he was considering buying his own ranch. He wasn't sure the family had believed him.

"Seriously, dude. After my accident, the money helped. Hell, it saved us, and we appreciated it—"

"I know, Chad." Landon watched Kylie pull ingredients out of the pantry and fridge. She didn't look very happy. "Listen, I'll call you later, huh?"

"Yeah, I gotta go too," Chad said, and Landon could hear all kinds of commotion in the background. "And dude, don't be a dumb ass. You might be able to pull off a bench seat, and hell, you can buy a table kit. But you don't need a broken hand to go with your leg. Not if you want to make it to the finals."

"I hear you." They disconnected, and Landon limped closer to Kylie. "You need some help?"

"Do you know how to frost cupcakes so they'll all come out identical?"

He rubbed his jaw. "Can't say as I've done it before, but if you showed me…"

She smiled. "I was teasing." She glanced down at his leg, and when she looked up again the smile was gone. "And by the way, just because you had a clever idea doesn't mean I didn't notice that you just had to stick your nose in my meeting with Joe. Even after I asked you to stay out of it."

"Um, excuse me, but you only told me to stay in the kitchen. And secondly, I didn't say a word to him."

"So hovering in the doorway had nothing to do with this idea of yours?"

"You mean the *clever* idea?"

"I said it was a decent idea," she muttered, and bent over to look in a lower cabinet. "But I haven't said I approve of you doing any of the work."

"True." From where he was standing he had a great view of her rear. The worn denim stretched over the curve of her perfect behind, making him itch where he most definitely couldn't scratch.

"So you honestly think you could build two bench booths? In your condition?" she asked as she straightened with a large platter in hand. Staring at him with a slight frown, she paused. "And that it wouldn't cost all that much?"

Clearing his throat, Landon turned to lean against the island. He didn't think she'd caught him eyeing her butt, but couldn't be sure. "How did you find Joe? Someone must've recommended him."

She nodded. "It was Sadie. I trust that he probably gave me an honest price if that's what you're getting at. It's just more than I expected." She peeked inside the commercial oven that looked older than dirt. "At least I don't have to do everything at once. I can have it done in stages."

"I wouldn't offer to help if I thought I couldn't do it."

"You're serious?"

"Piece of cake." The words were barely out of his mouth and he started to sweat.

The excitement he saw in her eyes lasted all of ten seconds before she shook her head. "It would take too long and you need to rest your leg."

"I've got two weeks to kill. That's more than enough time. I wouldn't know how to tackle the counter." Landon's thoughts were zipping all over the map. There had to be a way to do this without making a complete ass of himself, but he had to slow down, think before opening his big mouth again. "Joe can have that job so you won't worry about taking the work from him."

Kylie's lips tilted up. "Smarty. Think you know me that well?"

"Yeah, actually."

"You're right," she said with a soft laugh. "It would've bothered me." She eyed his injured leg before picking up the spatula. "I honestly think this is a bad idea."

"I swear I won't be stupid about it. I want to make the finals more than anything. Hell, I want to win the whole thing and that won't happen with a bum leg."

"Gold buckle fever?" she said with a touch of sarcasm.

"Sure, that would be nice. But it's really about the prize money. Not to mention the endorsement deals. That kind of dough is life-changing."

Kylie straightened her spine again, then bowed her head, pretending to stir the frosting. He wanted to kick himself. How many times had Gary said that to her? Letting her think the picket fence was just around the corner. The bastard hadn't even made it past the first round of the finals when he'd started screwing any woman who'd hit on him.

"Kylie?"

"What?" She wouldn't look up.

"I promise you I won't do anything that might hurt my leg."

"That's what you say, but—"

"Have I ever lied to you before?"

Her hesitation pissed him off, but he managed to keep his cool. Kylie thought he should've told her about what Gary was doing behind her back. But Landon's motives wouldn't have been pure and she knew that. She'd still been with Gary, which placed him in a tricky position. Regardless, he had never lied to her, not even when Gary had asked him to cover for him. He refused to think about how many times he'd simply kept quiet.

With a defiant jut of her chin, she finally looked up. "I have no way of knowing that, do I?"

"You can choose to believe me," he said, holding her gaze steady. "Just like I choose to trust that you're always truthful with me."

Kylie blinked and a light blush stained her cheeks. Yeah, that didn't make him wonder if she was thinking about the day he'd almost kissed her. The day they'd come close to admitting their feelings for each other. And then backed off.

As for giving her the impression he knew anything about building furniture, he'd get help, but he wanted the finished product to be a surprise, that's all.

"You didn't let me finish." She turned away and plucked a fresh dish towel out of a drawer. "I wasn't implying that you'd lie, but that you might push too hard without realizing it and set back your recovery."

"That's always a possibility no matter what I'm doing. I'm just saying I'd be extra careful."

"Anyway, the counter is more important to me than the extra seating," she said. "So if they have to wait it wouldn't be so terrible."

"I would've thought it was the other way around."

"What I haven't mentioned to anyone besides Rachel and Mallory is that I'm hoping to eventually make the place more like a real coffee bar." She glanced toward the front and lowered her voice. "Of course I can only offer a small selection of specialty coffees, but the profit margin on those kinds of drinks will be a big help."

"You really think you'll have enough customers? I can't see the locals paying five bucks for a latte."

"Actually, I'm mostly counting on the guests from the Sundance. They're always asking about the nearest Starbucks. But you'd be surprised at how many cowboys come in looking for fancy coffee drinks."

Landon held back a snort. There was no way those guys were coming in for coffee. "What's the Sundance?"

"The McAllisters' ranch. Rachel's family owns it."

"A dude ranch?"

"Depends on who you ask," Kylie said, grinning. "They've raised cattle for several generations. But when the economy got dicey Rachel turned an unused portion of the house into guest quarters. It's been super successful so she's stuck with it. Her brothers still run the cattle operation."

"Must be a big spread."

"Close to four thousand acres, I think."

He let out a low whistle.

"Isn't your family's ranch almost that size?"

"About half that, enough to keep my brothers and a full-time hired man busy."

"You have two brothers, right? Chad and...?"

"Martin."

"It sounds like a lot of work," she said, frowning.

"They hire seasonal help when they need it. Lots of teenagers look for summer work in the area."

"They must miss you. I bet they can't wait for you to quit the rodeo and join them."

Landon shrugged. "I don't know, they're doing pretty well without me."

For the second time today, one of them was saved by the bell.

Kylie groaned even before she turned to see who it was. "I'll be right with you, Mrs. Perkins," she said with a bright smile.

"Take your time, dear. I'm in no hurry."

"Great," Kylie mumbled under her breath. "I'm never going to finish these cupcakes in time. That woman can talk my ear off."

"Let me help her. If I have a question, I'll ask you."

Staring at him, Kylie set down the spatula. "Are you serious?"

"Why not?" He shrugged. "How hard can it be?"

Kylie laughed, then tried covering it up by clearing her throat. "Not hard at all."

Two hours and five customers later, Landon realized he should've paid more attention to the way Kylie had laughed and not what she'd said. The senior ladies of Blackfoot Falls could put the military's best interrogators to shame.

At least, in the few minutes he'd had without a customer, he'd convinced her to have dinner with him. But first he needed to find Joe Hopkins and propose a deal that would earn him some extra cash, assuming he could keep the arrangement to himself.

UNTIL FIVE MINUTES before she left to meet Landon, Kylie had considered wearing the second dress Rachel had badgered her into buying. Then she saw reason. The semi-sexy dress would send the wrong message. This wasn't a date. Tonight was nothing more than two old friends catching up.

She did wear her good jeans, though. And a relatively new green knit top. After all, they were going to the steakhouse and not the diner.

At 5:30 p.m., the evening air was already nippy as she hurried toward Main Street. A few trucks were parked in front of the Full Moon Saloon. After the dinner hour, it would be much busier. As she came around the corner, she saw Landon standing outside the restaurant. She slowed her steps even as her heart picked up speed.

She loved it when he wore blue shirts—any shade. They always made his eyes look bluer and, with his wavy dark hair, he truly was a good-looking man. A fact many of the other riders' wives and girlfriends had certainly noticed. And the female fans? They always mobbed him after events. Which said something considering there'd been a long stretch where he wasn't ranked and hadn't earned any big money. Although she did recall Gary mentioning something about Landon being a fool for taking a whole year off, even if it was for family, because of how well he'd been doing. So maybe that was part of the reason he attracted the buckle bunnies. Yet she'd never seen him flirt. Not once. She wondered why that was.

As soon as he spotted her, he headed toward her. "You walked?"

"I live less than ten minutes away. Where are your crutches?"

"I thought we were going right in to dinner so I didn't need them."

"And yet, here you are," she said, shaking her head. "Not smart, Landon."

"We can fix that. Come here."

"What?"

"Put your arm around my waist," he said at the same time as he slid an arm around her shoulders and leaned against her slightly.

At first she couldn't speak. He smelled so good. Felt too good. The warmth of his body seeped into hers, beckoning her closer. He was all lean muscle. Rock solid. But she'd already known that from the time he'd gotten bucked hard against the rails and she'd wrapped his bruised ribs. He'd refused to see a doctor, just like all the other rodeo idiots.

"Is the leg bothering you?" she asked, tightening her arm around him.

"Not especially."

Suspicious, she looked up at him. "So why are we plastered to each other?"

"Hmm. Well, speaking for myself, I like it."

Kylie rolled her eyes to hide the giddiness zipping through her. Even as they made it to the door of the restaurant, she didn't let go…and then her phone beeped. It was Kevin. Fate? No, karma.

"Go on and take that if you want." Landon lowered his arm. "I'll get us a table."

"I'll just be a second," she said, then answered. "Hi."

"Hey, you. Did you get some sleep? Hope I didn't keep you out too late," Kevin said with a laugh, since he'd teased her about having an early curfew.

Landon opened the door, then stepped back to let an older couple exit. The timing could've been better. Though she didn't care if he knew it was Kevin. Or heard any of her conversation. Why should she?

The couple looked like so many tourists who'd been stopping in Blackfoot Falls over the summer months. The man nodded and the woman smiled at Landon. "Thank you, young man," the wife said.

"Kylie?"

"Yes? Oh, I'm fine. Went right to sleep."

And of course someone else followed directly behind them. She couldn't catch a break.

"I had a great time last night," Kevin said, dropping his voice.

Kylie smiled at the second couple and moved closer to the curb to give them all room. "Me too."

Kevin paused. "You sound—hey, sorry. I should've asked if this was a good time."

"Actually, I'm about to have dinner with Landon," she said and was met with silence. "He said thanks for the discount." She saw his little smile as he ducked his head to see if anyone else was coming.

"Yeah, no problem."

"I'll call you later, okay?"

"Sure. And if you're free Saturday night?" Kevin asked. "We'll talk when you call."

"Yep. Thanks." She realized she'd sounded awfully abrupt and shouldn't have been so quick to disconnect. But like so many things in her life, it was too late.

Chapter Seven

The steakhouse was small, dimly lit and crowded. A middle-aged woman welcomed them with a smile and a surprised look at Kylie before she showed them to the last vacant booth.

"If you'd prefer a table, we have those two over there near the window," the hostess said, gesturing with the menu.

"This is fine, Irene, thanks." Kylie darted a look at him. "I assume this is okay with you."

"Anywhere you want."

As they slid onto the black vinyl seat, Irene laid the menus on the table. "Glad to see you finally made it in here to eat, Kylie."

"It's a special occasion." She glanced at Landon. "I have a friend visiting from out of town," she said and made a quick introduction.

After the woman left with their drink orders, Kylie glanced around at the signage and pictures on the walls, all from a long-ago era. "It's nice, isn't it?" she said. "Rustic and cozy." Landon nodded, but he couldn't pull his gaze away from Kylie. Her hair was down, all shiny with some bounce to it, and skimming her shoulders every time she turned her head. Being able to look at her across the table, watch the way her eyes sparkled had its advantages. Even though he would've preferred her sitting closer to him. Hopefully that time would come soon.

Last night, lying in bed, unable to sleep, he'd done a lot of thinking. When he'd first met Kylie, four years ago, she'd always been quick to help any busted-up cowboy Gary brought home, Landon included.

And then two years ago, she'd stopped. At least with him. He knew why, of course. That day when she'd been so upset because some strange woman kept calling for Gary…it had been the beginning of a long and painful time for her. That day, though, he'd somehow ended up with her alone in the house, and he'd itched to comfort her. And tell her the truth about Gary, but how could he, when he wanted her so badly for himself? She'd find out, and she'd hate him for it.

Instead, he'd pulled her into a hug, something he should never have done. She'd moved back just enough to look him in the eyes. Her own had been red from crying, but she was still beautiful to him. When her lips had parted, he'd leaned down…

They'd both come to their senses before they'd crossed that final line. He'd left, hating himself. After that, she'd continued to patch up the other guys but she'd always seemed to have an excuse to avoid him.

Now, after seeing her again, he still believed that long-ago attraction had been real, even if she truly hadn't given him a thought since she'd left. But she'd admitted he made her heart race. It was a start.

He focused on her smile. "Why haven't you been in here? This is the only restaurant in town besides the diner, right?"

"Yes, but they haven't been open that long. The owners had another restaurant here years ago, apparently, but closed it. Anyway, I don't eat out much. Other than going to barbeques at the Sundance and the Lone Wolf." She opened the menu and her eyes widened. "Oh, look at all these choices. I'll never be able to decide."

Landon smiled at her enthusiasm and let her look at the selections in peace. But right after Irene brought his beer and an iced tea for Kylie, he asked the question that had been nagging at him. "So, were you trying to make Kevin jealous, or trying to brush him off?"

Kylie looked up, her eyes narrowing. "What on earth are you talking about?"

"Earlier, when you told him you were having dinner with me."

"It's no big deal. You're an old friend. He knows that."

"Ouch," he said, and smiled. "I think we've moved past the denials, don't you?" A blink was her only response. "I'm pretty sure you knew that I was attracted to you from the first minute we met. But you were with Gary, so I kept to myself…or at least I tried to. Go ahead and tell me if I'm wrong, but I think you felt something too."

Kylie blinked again, then briefly looked away. "Okay. I'll admit, there were sparks. But honestly, Landon, I never let myself think about it. Especially when everything went to hell with Gary. It just felt wrong…" She put the menu down and folded her hands over it. "Ever since I left Iowa, I've been determined to give myself a decent life. A real home of my own, start a business, even though it cost every penny I had. I've built my life here one brick at a time. One that's safe, that I can be proud of."

It killed him to ask, but he had to. "And Kevin fits into that life?"

She didn't answer right away. "To tell you the truth, I barely know Kevin. He hasn't even reached friend status yet."

Landon cleared his throat, but met her eyes squarely. "Do you think you might want to entertain the idea that there could be something between us?"

She inhaled, although she had to realize he wasn't just going to turn tail and run. "I don't know," she said. "And that's as honest as I can be."

"Mind if I stick around until you do?" he asked softly.

Kylie looked down at her hands, and he noticed her cheeks flush. When she looked at him again, she said, "I can't say when that will be."

"Fair enough." He smiled, knowing he'd take whatever she'd give him.

She nibbled at her lip, opened her menu again. "Have you ever had trout before?"

Landon hadn't thought Kevin was anyone to worry about but now that he knew, he'd take it into account. He just wished he was more certain about his own future. "My brothers and I used to catch trout by the bucket loads every summer. Had to clean the suckers, too, or my mom wouldn't touch them. She'd pan fry them or put 'em in the smoker. By August I was damn sick of trout no matter how they were cooked."

She smiled. "How is your family?"

"They're all doing well. Working hard and giving me crap because I'm not there helping get ready for winter."

"You'd miss it if they didn't."

"Ha. Try me."

Kylie grinned. "Now, I have a question for you. Where are you in your plan? I think you have one more year, right?"

"My plan?"

"Your five-year plan?" She looked confused…no, more like upset. "When we first met, you said you had a five-year plan… You know, about leaving the rodeo next year and going back to Wyoming. To join your brothers?"

"Well, things have changed some since I made that decision, especially in this last year. And circumstances have changed at home too. Basically, everything's up in the air at this point…"

Kylie stared at him as if he'd just told her the sun would never shine again.

He wanted to stop talking, but it wasn't fair of him not to explain. At least about the things he knew. "Now that I'm doing so well in the rankings, I need to put away as much money as I can. So…I guess the short answer is, yes, I do plan to go back to ranching, but I'm not so sure about the rest of the picture."

"It's just that you were so adamant," she said with a shrug and looked down, although he doubted she was still studying the menu. "Does your family know you're here? I mean this close to Wyoming?"

"They know about my leg and that I'm sidelined, but I might've left out the part that I'm six hours away."

Kylie winced. At least he thought that's what that was.

"That's not very nice."

"They don't need me. And they're used to my schedule taking me all over the place. Mom's away visiting my sister in Utah. After she's back, I'll swing by on my way to Oklahoma."

"To a rodeo?"

He shook his head. "My doctor."

Relieved that they'd veered to a safer subject, he leaned back and drank his beer.

Irene returned with a pad and pencil. "You two ready?"

Kylie looked at the woman as if she were speaking Martian. "May we have another minute?"

"Take all the time you want, hon," Irene said. "I'll check back later, but feel free to give me a holler."

Kylie went back to studying the menu, and Landon almost teased her that she wasn't going to be quizzed. But he had a feeling it wasn't food that was on her mind. She was disappointed in him. Why, he wasn't sure. Maybe because he hadn't stuck to the plan? Or did it have something to do with him not seeing his family? Oh, hell, maybe it had nothing to do with him.

"Know what you want?" he asked.

"I think so. You?"

"Yep. Let's order so we can discuss your remodeling plans."

Kylie sighed. "I still think it's a bad idea."

"Why? You don't trust me?"

"You know why."

"You're not my mother, Kylie. Stop acting like it." Landon hadn't raised his voice, but he regretted his words.

She lowered her gaze and wouldn't look at him.

"I'm sorry, Kylie. I didn't mean that the way it sounded."

"No need to apologize. You're right." She gave him a fleeting smile that didn't reach her eyes.

Irene showed up again and Kylie ordered quickly, even adding a glass of wine. Which made him feel more like crap. He might've seen her drink alcohol maybe five times over the years.

While it was no excuse for his remark, he felt edgy, once again worried about pulling off this harebrained plan of his. Luckily he'd found Joe easily. They worked out some logistics and timeline, but Landon didn't know the guy from Adam. There was no way to be sure he wouldn't open his mouth, even though Landon was paying him to keep their deal private.

"Landon?"

Both women were looking expectantly at him. Irene had her pencil poised.

"Rib eye, medium rare, and a potato, nothing on it."

"Salad comes with it," Irene said. "We have some good homemade dressings."

"You know what, skip the potato. I do want a salad, but not the regular side." He quickly scanned the menu options. "I'd like the house special without the croutons and Italian dressing on the side."

Irene hesitated. "That's a big salad. People normally order it as an entrée."

"Good. Exactly what I want."

Grinning, Irene picked up the menus. "A man who watches his figure. How refreshing."

He was glad to see Kylie smile too.

"What?" he said, playing it up and patting his belly. "I'm not getting enough exercise with this bum leg. Gotta cut calories."

"Except for the occasional chocolate cupcake?" Kylie asked, before both women laughed, and Irene went to another table.

"You always were a healthy eater," Kylie said. "That's why I could never understand why you drank so much beer."

Landon was speechless for a moment. "When did you ever see me drink too much?"

"Um, the night you and Gary ended up in Mexico?"

"Ah." He nodded, pissed at himself just thinking about his stupidity. "It's something I try to forget." He stared into Kylie's beautiful eyes, and momentarily got off track. "Other than that night, did you ever see me drunk?"

Without stopping to think about it she shook her

head. "Actually, I've never seen you drink more than two beers."

"Sounds about right."

"Why that night?"

He shrugged, despite knowing the exact reason. "I'd just come back after my brother's accident." He paused while Irene delivered Kylie's wine.

"I don't think I ever heard what happened to him."

"It was a freak accident. He was trying to cut a calf loose from some barbed wire, and he fell down a twenty-foot slope. Martin didn't find him for over an hour. He didn't move him, instead they waited for the paramedics. The doctor said Chad was lucky. He could have been in much worse shape. He was in rehab for a long time, though. So I stayed to help Martin…" He realized he hadn't talked to anyone about this before. "Anyway, getting back on the circuit was harder than I expected."

"Gary and I had just met you around that time. I've always admired you for putting your family first."

"Hell, if I'd really put them first, I would've quit rodeoing altogether."

Kylie's lips parted. But she just blinked, didn't say a word.

He wanted to kick himself from here to next week for saying that, especially after everything he'd told her. He gulped some of his beer, wishing he knew if explaining he didn't mean it would help. That his brothers had sworn that he didn't need to stick around, and Martin had even said that his leaving might've been the best thing for Chad.

Kylie was studying him in a way that made him brace for more questions, ones that he wouldn't know how to answer. Before she could start, he said, "Let's talk about the bench seats."

She hesitated, but only for a second. "Oh, I didn't tell you. Joe called—the man who'd given me the quote? He gave me a different price for just the counter and condiment cabinet. It's totally within my budget and he's starting day after tomorrow."

"Great. I assume he's going to work after hours?"

"Mostly. But I offered to close a few half days as long as I can give my regular customers notice."

Landon did all he could to keep his annoyance from showing. "What did he say?"

"He liked that idea, especially since he still has to order some of the materials."

Damn, the old buzzard was already going off script. Great. Just great.

Irene brought their salads and the timing couldn't have been better. After she left, Landon said, "I'll have to place an order for the oak. I assume everyone uses the local hardware store?"

"You still want to take on the tables as well as the bench seats?" she asked softly. "Because honestly, I can wait."

"Why? I'm here."

"And another thing, I don't know where you'd be able to work."

"Do you have a garage?"

She nodded. "It's small, though. And you'd need tools... I don't have anything other than a hammer and screwdriver."

"I have some tools in my truck. Whatever else I need I'll pick up at the hardware store."

"You could probably borrow stuff from Matt. Or the McAllisters. You'd like them a lot."

"Maybe. I'll figure out what's what first."

After they'd each taken a few bites of their salads,

Kylie set her fork down and took a sip of wine. She made a little bit of a face, which Landon pretended not to notice.

"Promise me something," she said.

"What's that?"

"If the project gets to be too much for you, or it bothers your leg, or you get antsy to leave, please tell me. Don't—"

"Antsy to leave? I'm not going anywhere, Kylie." He held her gaze. Didn't she understand what he'd been trying to tell her? "I mean, I've got the doctor and I need to get back on the circuit, but I'm here for you."

"I just don't want you to feel as if you have to finish," she said.

Damn. Sticking to the year's grace period hadn't been easy. But he'd known she needed the time and space to heal, to fully understand that the failure was Gary's and not hers. But what had tormented him the most was the possibility she and Gary would reconcile. Landon had lost too much sleep worried that her guilt over their shared attraction would push her into giving Gary a second chance.

Kylie reached over and laid her hand on his. "Promise me?"

He sucked in a breath, and turned his hand over so that their palms met. "I promise."

Eyes wide and startled, she nodded. He barely had time to squeeze her hand before she retreated. "I've heard the hardware store has a problem bringing in special orders quickly. All this might be a moot point."

"That's crazy. What about Kalispell? That's what, less than an hour away? I bet we could get whatever we need there. What time do you close tomorrow?"

"Um, four o'clock."

"Okay, that's not bad if we leave right away."

Her brows went up. "We?"

"Well, yeah. I know oak is the front-runner, but you might find another kind of wood you like. Something that's cheaper. Any chance you can close an hour earlier?"

"I suppose," she said, stabbing at a cherry tomato.

"Another thing… Have you thought about the bar stools?" Landon waited for her to answer. But she sure wasn't in any hurry. "I guess I'm not clear on what you're aiming for."

"I'm not sure myself." She glanced around and lowered her voice. "It probably seems silly, but I can't alienate the townspeople."

"I get it. The town I'm from isn't all that much bigger than Blackfoot Falls."

"Seriously?" Kylie said, looking adorably baffled. "I don't think you told me that before. Huh." She stared at him for so long he considered hitting the restroom just to check if there was anything in his teeth. "While we're on the subject, why don't you have a girlfriend?"

He waited for the punch line. Evidently there wasn't one. "You do realize we weren't within a thousand miles of that subject."

"Don't be silly. It comes under the heading of stuff I don't know about you."

"Ah. Of course." He stalled, wondering what had prompted the question. He'd already told her he hadn't forgotten about her, but he didn't dare go overboard about that. Not yet. "Do you mean ever, or now?"

"Both."

"Aren't you forgetting about Sierra?"

Kylie wrinkled her nose. "You dated her for less than a month."

"Yeah, but we—" He cleared his throat, pretty sure

Kylie didn't expect him to be *that* honest. "We went out like six times."

She gave him a patient smile. "That's not what I meant and you know it."

"I'm only twenty-eight. Not exactly over the hill."

"I didn't ask why you weren't married."

He sipped his beer, not sure what else to say. Was she trying to throw up obstacles? "I had a girlfriend for the two years I was in college. Shelly wanted a city life, and I didn't. Can I eat my salad now?"

"I forgot you went to college. What was your major?"

"History," he said. "But I quit early."

Irene showed up with their meals. Landon quickly dug into his steak. A lot of chewing meant less talking. Kylie had opened a door. Maybe it was only by a crack, but he was willing to do whatever it took to prove he was the right man for her.

Chapter Eight

Landon tensed when he noticed the time. He was supposed to pick Kylie up in twenty minutes for their trip to Kalispell. "Okay, let me explain this again." He'd been on the phone with Joe for a while and wasn't at all confident the guy understood the problem. Or the plan he'd gone over several times. "If Kylie closes the bakery early so you can work on the counter, that ups the chances of me being caught with my pants down."

"How do ya figure?"

His head was going to explode. He yanked a shirt out of the small closet and sent two hangers banging against the wall. "Because I'll be working in her garage. If she leaves early she'll probably go home."

He gave that a moment to sink in, but he wasn't counting on it. "And the deal was," he continued, "that you're supposed to be helping me during the day, then working on the counter in the evening—"

"Now hold on. I thought you said you were hiring me as a consultant."

"That's right. A *hands-on* consultant. With my bum leg, I don't know how much help I'll need." Landon knew he was stretching the truth some, but he couldn't admit he wasn't all that good with anything beyond a hammer.

"Ain't bad enough you're stealing the job right out

from under me. Now you're asking me to work twelve-hour days. And just when we're coming on hunting season."

Landon bit off a curse. "Joe, stop. Think about it for a minute. I'm paying you more than you quoted Kylie. You're ahead on this no matter how you look at it."

Joe was quiet a moment. "I can't figure out what you're getting out of this."

"Kylie's a friend and I want her to be happy. That's all. Look, can we just agree the project will be completed in two weeks? Delay the counter if you need to."

"I don't know about that. Kylie seemed more interested in getting the counter done first."

"Because she can't afford—" Landon had no business getting frustrated. Guilt pricked his conscience. He didn't want to mess things up for Kylie just because he'd bitten off more than he could chew. Even asking to work in her garage had been self-serving. He needed to spend more time with her. "You're right," Landon said. "The last thing I want to do is disappoint her."

Joe's rusty chuckle grated on his nerves. "You're sweet on her."

Landon sighed. "Yep."

"Why didn't you just say so, boy? Kylie's a good kid. I like her, so here's what we'll do. You go ahead and use her garage to distress the wood and seal it. My workshop's a few miles outside of town. That's where we'll do most of the construction."

By the time Landon had gotten the dimensions he'd need to get started and they finally disconnected he felt a lot better. All the sneaking around didn't sit well with him, except for the fact that Kylie would end up happy.

He slipped on his shirt, and since he had a few minutes, he decided to call Chad. Run a few things by him, go over the list before he and Kylie headed out.

"If it isn't the master carpenter."

Landon thought about hanging up on his brother, but decided it was better to just take the abuse. "Are you done? Or have you been saving up waiting for me to call."

"Both. What's up?"

"I have a list of stuff to get, and I want to make sure I'm not forgetting anything."

"Shoot."

"Oak for the bench seats and tables. Polyurethane for the—"

"Hold on. I did a little checking. Oak isn't your best bet. With the humidity in that part of the country, I'd go for ash or maple."

Landon should have done his own research, dammit. He had done some internet searches to see what he was getting himself into, but he hadn't considered humidity. In fact, Joe hadn't said anything either. "Is that going to make a big difference?"

"Depends on how long you want the furniture to last."

"Okay. Good. Thanks." He continued down the list, most of which he'd gotten from Joe, the rest from the DIY websites he'd found.

Chad waited until he was finished. "Sounds good. But I know what you generally keep in your toolbox. You realize you'll need things like a router, circular saw, a power drill—"

"I'm using someone's workshop. He's got all that stuff."

"Okay, that just leaves the tool belt."

Landon was just about to ask what kind when he heard Chad's wife call out, "Women *love* tool belts. Make sure it rides low on your hips."

Chad laughed. "Cindy's right. And don't skimp on the leather. You gonna tell me who she is or what?"

Landon sighed. "She's a friend."

"A friend? Try again, dude. You aren't doing this for a pal."

"Fine. She's a really good friend. And that's it, I'm not saying anything else."

Sounding a little distanced, as if he'd turned away from the phone, Chad said, "It's definitely serious."

"Dammit, Chad. Knock it off. And tell Cindy I can hear her whooping it up back there. Jeez."

"Okay, okay. You're helping a buddy. Spending a lot of time and money on furniture that you could buy anywhere, instead of risking a hell of a lot by acting like you know what you're doing."

"Chad…"

"Look, I'm not saying don't do it. But building this stuff isn't like putting up a prefab shed or fixing fences. Nobody's better when it comes to breaking horses. But carpentry?"

"Which is why I'm calling you. You can build damn near anything, and I figure if I run into trouble, I can count on your help. Right?"

"Hey, if it's important to you, it's important to me. Tell what. I'll text you a list of everything you should need to get this sucker done, okay? You can match it to what you already have."

The relief Landon felt was immense. "Thanks. I'll call you later."

"Wait. I'm putting this on the list, but just to be clear, make sure you have a level. And you know how to use it."

"Come on. I'm not an idiot. 'Course I have a level."

"'Course you do. Talk to you later."

Landon clicked off the call, then right after he added *low-riding tool belt* to his list, he wrote *level*.

KYLIE SWAPPED THE Closed sign for the one she'd put out first thing in the morning, letting people know she was closing an hour early. She'd lived in Blackfoot Falls long enough that she should've expected the barrage of questions. But the degree of some people's nosiness still amazed her.

Just what she needed, too. After yesterday's conversation with Landon she could barely keep a thought in her head. He actually wanted to take their relationship to a new level. The idea had brought up all kinds of feelings she'd tried to forget. How much she liked him, the role he'd played in her fantasies for longer than she should admit. The fact was, she based a lot of her new criteria for the kind of man she wanted on Landon. His kindness, consideration and so much more.

But it bothered her that he hadn't remembered his plan. Landon had always seemed like such a solid guy who knew exactly what he wanted. Obviously, he'd changed. And while she knew he wasn't Gary, not knowing how long he'd be rodeoing and being unsure about where he'd end up were big obstacles. Especially after this incredibly difficult year she'd spent building the life she had now.

Stepping out onto the sidewalk, she peered in the direction of the motel. No sign of Landon yet, although she had a few minutes before they were going to meet. What the heck, she'd use it to touch up her makeup.

"Hey, Kylie…"

Mallory's voice stopped her at the door. She ducked her head and saw Mallory locking up the Full Moon. It wouldn't open for another three hours.

"Got a minute?" Mallory asked, briskly walking toward her.

"Sure. What's up?"

"First, Landon. Wow." Mallory was wearing her usual jeans and T-shirt, her hair pulled into a messy ponytail, and she still looked gorgeous. It just didn't seem fair. "I mean, holy crap. How come you never mentioned him?"

"I'm sure I know a lot of people I've never mentioned," Kylie said, grinning at Mallory's glare.

"Let me be more specific. Hot guys who're hot for you. Got a lot of them stashed away?"

"Okay, I agree he's hot. But we're just…"

"Friends?" Mallory studied her with a question in her eyes, though not for long. One of the things Kylie liked about her was that she wasn't nosy. She wouldn't ask why Kylie was suddenly wearing makeup to work. "Also, Rachel's off sweets. Her doc thinks her new obsession with sugar is causing her recent mood swings."

"Oh, no. Poor Rach. Although she has been over-indulging."

Mallory let out a laugh. "That's putting it nicely. She's been inhaling sweets like they're going to run out." She glanced down Main Street. "My car's in the shop. Gunner is picking me up. Anyway, if she comes to the bakery, don't give her anything, no matter how much she begs."

"What? I'm supposed to cut her off? And expect to keep breathing? I don't think so."

"Hey, this comes from Rachel herself."

Something didn't feel right. "Okay, why didn't she call and tell me?" Kylie said. "I'm practically her dealer."

"According to Sally, Rachel just got the news yesterday and she's in mourning." Mallory's gaze drifted beyond Kylie. "I think your *just friend* is here," she said with a barely contained laugh.

"Really, Mallory?" Kylie gave her a quick glare before glancing back to see Landon pulling to the curb. "Here I thought you were better than that."

"I know, right? Guess I've been living here too long."

They both laughed. And then Kylie had the sudden urge to tell Mallory about last night. What Landon had said, and how she felt about it all. Kylie needed someone to be the voice of reason, and Mallory would give it to her straight. Though Kylie was still so unsure she'd probably muddle the whole conversation.

Landon powered down his window.

"I just have to grab my purse and lock the door," Kylie called to him, and he nodded. She met Mallory's gaze. "Behave."

"You're in luck," Mallory said, shading her eyes from the sinking sun. "I see Gunner's truck."

Kylie darted inside, took a quick look in the bathroom mirror and decided against lip gloss. In less than a minute she'd locked the front door and jiggled the knob for good measure.

Gunner had brought his truck to a stop in the middle of the street. Mallory headed toward him, while he seemed to be admiring Landon's truck.

Just as Kylie reached the passenger door, Gunner stuck his head out the window and yelled, "Hi, gorgeous. Had one of your éclairs last week. Damn, it was good."

"I heard you blamed me for the five extra miles you had to run the next day."

Gunner laughed. "True."

"See ya," Kylie tossed over her shoulder as she climbed into Landon's truck.

"Am I gonna have to start beating guys off with my crutches?"

"Oh, please." Kylie rolled her eyes, even as a little

shiver chased down her spine. "He and Mallory are a couple, and believe me, he doesn't have eyes for anyone but her."

Landon pulled out onto the road. "You say that guy's a runner?"

"Yeah, he is. Um, are we still going to Kalispell?"

"Isn't that what we decided?"

"I thought so." She pressed her lips together. "You should probably turn around."

"Oh, hell." He squinted at the highway sign as they left the town limits. "Don't laugh."

"I'm trying not to."

The side of his mouth hiked up. "Are there any side streets that might loop around? Or do I have to make a U-turn and go back through town?"

"Better go back down Main since it's the only way I know." A light flashed on the computerized dashboard screen. "You've always had a good sense of direction. This wouldn't be a ploy to show off your new truck?"

He grinned. "It's a beauty, isn't it? My old beater had finally started to give up. It stalled twice in one week, and I said, that's it. I coughed up some of the prize money I've been saving and drove this puppy off the lot. Besides, I got a deal too good to pass up."

Kylie had wondered about his truck. It must've cost a fortune, even with a deal. Which wasn't like Landon. He'd been sensible, if not frugal, which she'd admired. On the other hand, his old truck had been a real clunker.

As they passed Gunner's truck, she remembered Landon asking about him being a runner before they got sidetracked.

"Gunner used to work as a stuntman before he moved here last summer," Kylie said. "He still takes stunt jobs now and then, mostly when they're shooting a movie nearby. Mallory said it has something to do with keeping his union benefits. I guess he has to stay in shape for that. He runs almost every day."

"What does he do here?"

"He and another ex-stuntman are partners in a ranch. In fact, they raise and train animals for Hollywood. Horses mostly."

"But he's not from the area?"

"Nope."

"Huh. He looks young, but he just up and quit and moved out here. Good for him having an exit strategy."

Like the plan Landon had abandoned? "I don't think that was it." Kylie said, upset that she was pulling apart everything he said. If she wanted to give this an honest try, she'd have to give them both some leeway. "Mallory's from LA, but she got here around the time I did. They'd been friends for years and when Gunner came after her..." Seeing the question in Landon's eyes, she wished she'd phrased that differently. "Bottom line is they're together and very happy."

"Kind of a familiar story, don't you think?" Landon said with a slow, unnerving smile. "So, dinner first, or do you want to get the shopping over with?"

"You didn't say anything about dinner," she muttered, wondering if their story could turn out just as happy.

Chapter Nine

Even armed with the list Chad had sent him, walking into Home Depot made Landon uneasy. There was some comfort in the familiar layout of the store, although he'd rather be riding buck naked on a high roller than face the rows and rows of hardware. Especially while using crutches. He'd thought about leaving them in the truck, but they had a lot of walking on hard cement floor ahead of them.

"Wood first?" Kylie asked.

"Yep. Let's get one of those platform carts. And a regular one for the smaller stuff."

She insisted on pushing the flatbed, which, yes, okay, was necessary. That left him to maneuver with one crutch under his arm and the other tucked in the cart in order to give him a free hand. Kylie looked as if she was about to protest but met his eyes and didn't argue.

"I can't believe I forgot to tell you," she said, as they walked toward the back of the store. "I mentioned you needing a helper to Rachel, who told Matt, who then got in touch with some friends of his. He found a kid named Barry who's a high-school wrestler, which means he's pretty strong."

"No kidding?" Landon saw that his lack of enthusiasm didn't go unnoticed. But he would've preferred a kid her friends didn't know. Just in case this Barry let something slip. "That's great."

"It's not for sure."

"If it doesn't work out we'll find someone else."

"You know you can back out at any time, right?"

"Hey, I'm looking forward to this. I just don't want any of it to be an added burden on you."

"It was a phone call," she said, laughing. "Not to mention I'm the one benefiting from all this. Anyway, Joe's coming in at three tomorrow, so I won't have to close too early. Then I'm supposed to meet with the woman who wants part-time work. After that I'll be free to help do whatever you need."

Landon did a quick mental calculation. "Won't you have prep work to do for the next morning?"

"I'll try not to get in the way," she said, clearly disappointed. "But if you'd rather I stay out of your hair—"

"Hey." He stopped in the middle of the plumbing aisle and cupped her elbow. "All I'd planned to do was hang around and pester you until I was all healed up. And if you think this little project is going to keep me out of *your* hair, think again."

A faint blush and a shy smile encouraged him to slide his palm down her arm and give her hand a light squeeze. Her skin was so soft, her fingers small and delicate. This little trip to Home Depot wasn't turning out so bad after all.

And then her phone chirped and ruined the moment. Not that those few lousy seconds amounted to anything earth-shattering. "It's just a text," she said, her gaze lowering to the phone she'd pulled out of her pocket. "But I do need to check it."

"No problem."

Whatever she saw brought a smile to her lips. It

could've been Rachel confirming the kid was a go, or any one of her friends, for any number of reasons...

She finally looked up, but got distracted by something behind him.

He followed her gaze and found an orange-vested dude waving and racing toward them in one of the store's motorized scooters they had for people with disabilities. As if the crutches weren't bad enough.

At Kylie's laughter, he transferred his glare to her. "What?"

She bit her lip. "Your face."

"I'm glad you think this is funny."

"It won't be when his head explodes from the way you're looking at him. He's just trying to be nice."

By the time the kid reached them, he must've picked up on Landon's vibe because he didn't look quite so eager. He stopped the scooter a few feet away and looked from Landon to Kylie and back again.

"I appreciate the gesture." Landon kept his tone light with the boy, refusing to sound like Smaug, although if that cart didn't turn around right now, he might start breathing fire. "But I'm good."

"It doesn't cost anything. We keep them for customers who—" The boy's Adam's apple bobbed as he noisily cleared his throat. "Okay, sir. But if you need—"

"Turn that thing around. Now."

The kid disappeared before Landon's scowl did.

Kylie was still giggling, only now her cheeks were a deeper pink and her eyes were damp. "This is a new side to you."

"Oh, hell, can you see me riding around in one of those things?"

"Doesn't fit your macho image?"

"As a matter of fact…" His glare was wasted on her. "No."

The admission set her off again. "Come on, that was priceless."

"Hilarious," he said, and looked at his watch. Then her. Then his watch again.

"Fine. Go on ahead if you're so anxious. I have to find a tissue."

He hobbled away as quickly as he could without losing his balance or his dignity. Although that last one was already a goner.

BY THE TIME they reached the lumber, Kylie had pulled herself together. It hadn't been very nice to laugh at Landon, but honestly he'd asked for it. And she hadn't been kidding about seeing a new side to him. She wasn't sure what to make of it.

"You said oak?"

She nodded as she led him down the aisle with all the appearance boards. Everything from hardwoods to laminates.

"It's a decent wood."

Kylie slowed. "But?"

"Oak is a hardwood, but it's not going to last as long as something like ash or maple."

"Are you saying I'd have to replace it in a few years?"

"No, nothing like that. More than likely you won't have to worry about a thing. I'm just saying you should keep an open mind."

She ran her hand over the smooth surface. It was difficult to believe something that looked so strong had hidden weaknesses.

Moving onward, Kylie stopped by the ash samples,

which had that rustic look she liked, but was a little cheaper than the oak.

Mesmerized, she watched the way Landon stroked the lighter wood. They were big, his hands. Sturdy and calloused from hard work, helping at his family's ranch, even doing some chores for Kylie when her pleas to Gary had fallen on deaf ears during those last two awful years.

But she'd also seen Landon with horses, and the way he could gentle a tempestuous stallion was a sight to behold. It was difficult not to imagine those hands on her. Stroking the tension out of her muscles, easing her fears, her doubts…

A loudspeaker announcement jerked her out of her reverie, and she studied the wood as if it were the most fascinating thing ever. As her racing heart slowed enough to let her breathe again, she had to admit, his suggestion had merit. "Well, it is beautiful."

"Hey, I've been mulling something over… I wasn't sure when to bring it up, but I guess now's as good a time as any. What would you think about an investor?"

"In the bakery?"

"Well, yeah, now that you're expanding."

She knew exactly what he was doing, and she appreciated the gesture, but it sure left a sour taste in her mouth.

"Before you answer, just remember I meant it when I said I won't be rodeoing forever. I figure I have a couple more good years. After that…"

"Stop. I don't need your help. I'm doing fine. Besides, you told me last night you had to put away money for your future, not lend it out. At the moment, you're already helping me more than I ever expected with the furniture."

He looked as if he wanted to argue but just nodded, and she turned her attention to the wood, imagining what it would be like as a bench seat, as tables and chairs.

"Rachel suggested that maybe I could find some cute funky chairs at garage sales. That might make up for some of the extra expense. Because I do like this ash a lot," she said, "especially the durability. I plan on having that bakery for a long time."

"How long?" Landon asked, as if the answer actually mattered to him.

That was all it took to send her brain off in a thousand different directions. Yet the truth was, the question could mean nothing at all. "Um, at least until my next birthday," she said.

His mouth curved into a feeble smile. Guess he didn't appreciate her little joke. Or maybe all this wasn't simple for him, either.

"I'M GLAD WE decided to eat," Kylie said as they climbed back into the truck. "I think that just might've been the best burger I've ever had."

"Me too. And that strawberry shake. Man, I couldn't live near here." Landon started the engine and looked over at her when she laughed. "What's so funny?"

"You have the most self-control of anyone I've ever met."

"I don't know about that," he muttered and pulled out of the burger joint parking lot, heading for the highway.

She'd changed her mind about dinner after she'd gotten the text from Rachel. Matt and Trace McAllister had offered to meet them at her place to help unload the truck. She hadn't told Landon about the plan, but it was the sensible thing to do. He'd promised not to go overboard and she was just helping him keep that promise.

They ended up spending the drive discussing the pros and cons of upholstering the benches. By the time they reached Blackfoot Falls, she'd officially vetoed any upholstery. If people wanted cushioned butts, they could go hang out at the diner.

"What's this?" Landon asked, as he slowed down at her house. A truck was parked in her driveway off to the left.

"Matt and Trace are here to help unload," she said.

"Trace?"

"Rachel's brother."

"Why?"

She waited until Landon had backed up to the garage. "Because it'll take half the time and they volunteered."

"I'm not crippled, Kylie."

"Yeah, but who has the patience to watch you carry one board at a time? Come on. Let's get this done." She jumped out of the truck, hoping he'd drop his objections.

Trace, whom she didn't know well—only that he liked apple fritters more than was healthy—opened the garage door, and turned on the lights.

She saw the guys hadn't come empty-handed. "What's all this?" she asked, nodding at the stuff that hadn't been there that morning.

Matt walked out of the shadows. "Workbench, miter saw, jigsaw, router. If you need anything else, I'm sure someone around here has it."

Landon moved in next to her, without his crutches. "That's so nice," she said. "Landon, you know Matt Gunderson."

"We met at the San Antonio Stock Show a couple years ago." Landon stuck out his hand and the men shook.

"Sorry about your leg. Man, you've been flying up the ranks. Think you'll be ready for the finals?"

"If he doesn't hurt himself building all this furniture." Kylie went to the back of the truck and put down the gate. "Okay, guys, looks like I have to get up extra early to make you donuts and fritters. You're totally awesome. Oh, and Trace, introduce yourself."

"Yes, ma'am," Trace said, as he walked up to Landon and shook his hand. "Trace McAllister. Nice to meet you." Then he pulled four 2x4s from the truck bed and walked them into the corner of the garage while Matt moved the worktable out of the way.

Kylie's heart was pounding crazy fast. Landon had said he'd been doing well, but hearing *Matt* ask him about the finals? Somehow that made it seem more real.

"You know I could have taken care of this tomorrow," Landon said, leaning down so only she could hear.

"Yes. You could have. But you didn't need to do it on your own. Honestly, if this is about you being all macho, I swear I'll tell everyone about that electric scooter."

His frown was exactly what she'd expected. It didn't help that it made him look brooding and sexier than it should have. She slipped a wood panel out of the truck bed before she let her imagination run away with her, and carried it to the spot she'd cleared earlier. She'd also made sure the built-in utility shelves were mostly empty so Landon could keep his tools within easy reach.

After she unloaded, she returned to the truck and grabbed two more boards and slid them out until she could hoist them under her arms.

"Hey, hey," Landon said. "Let me do that. Those are heavy."

"I lift fifty-pound bags of flour on a regular basis. Don't sweat it."

"Yeah, Landon," Matt said, lifting three times the number of boards. "You should have seen her when she opened the store. No one messes with the cake whisperer."

"Sounds about right," Landon said, then passed her, no crutches, but with his arms full of trim molding.

After putting them in the corner, he looked around the garage while she watched him. He exhaled heavily and lost the furrowed brow. From then on, things ran like clockwork, and before she knew it, Matt and Trace were saying their goodbyes.

"Don't forget," she called after them. "Free donuts and fritters for a week."

"Thanks," Matt said, looking serious. "But none for Rachel."

"I'll take care of her share of the fritters," Trace said, grinning.

"Okay, I'll be sure to let your sister know about your kind offer." Kylie laughed at his stricken expression.

She and Landon stood shoulder-to-shoulder as they watched Matt back his truck onto the street. After a final wave, Landon ran his fingers softly up her arm. It was a wisp of a move, nothing that would have meant a thing if it had come from, say, Kevin, but it gave her goose bumps.

"That was nice of them to help. But I can tell you did a lot of prep before we got here. You always did like a clean work space," he said, almost as if he were talking to himself. "It used to piss me off how those guys that hung out at your place were such inconsiderate jerks."

"Remind me to thank your mother, should I ever meet her," Kylie said. "You were always very polite."

"It was both my folks, really. We learned our manners straight off, and while we each had our minor rebellions during our teens, it was never anything crazy."

Somehow they were standing even closer to each other. So close, she had to look up to meet his gaze. She wanted him to touch her. To give her that little electric charge. But he didn't.

"You should get inside. It's getting late." His gaze

roamed over her face, as if he was mapping her from the top of her head to her lips, to her eyes, then her lips again.

Turned out his touch didn't need to be physical.

"How about you come in and I give you a drink before I kick you out?"

"A quick one would be good," he said. "You really have to get up at four every morning?"

"Yep. Curse of being a baker." She smiled and led him into the house, his uneven steps, one foot, one crutch, right behind.

After flipping on the kitchen light, she went straight to the fridge. "Beer? I have some wine that I haven't tried, orange juice and, uh…" She shifted the milk to the side "…coconut water."

"Coconut water?"

"It's good. Want to try some?"

"I'll take your word for it. A beer sounds just right."

"Chicken," she said, handing him a bottle, and taking one for herself. She knew she wouldn't finish it, but that was okay. Just a little would help her fall asleep. Maybe stop her overactive thoughts from going to unhealthy places.

He opened both beers, and followed her to the living room. She turned on the side table lamps, which gave the room a soft glow. The couch was something she'd found at an estate sale, and it had become one of her favorite things. It was a beautiful sea green, well built and curved so one side was long enough to be able to stretch out for a nap.

Landon had walked over to the bookshelves, where she also had placed a few pictures. There were a couple of her grandparents, some of the friends she'd made since moving in. Nothing much from her old life.

She sat on the smaller side of the couch, so he could stretch out his leg easily.

Instead, he sat next to her, leaning the crutch to his right.

The smart thing to do would be to move over. Keep her distance. For now, anyway. He'd certainly given her enough to consider before she put her heart on the line. Plus her impulses weren't all that trustworthy when it came to Landon.

Stupid hormones. Stupid handsome cowboy.

So why wasn't she turning away from his darkening gaze? In the quiet room, she could hear his breathing as he leaned toward her, the warmth from his thigh breaching the denim of her jeans.

"Kylie…"

The whisper was just as potent as his touch had been. Only worse, because his breath teased her lips and heated her cheek. Or maybe that was just the blush of want that was making her forget herself.

She blinked. And that split second was enough to remind her of what was at stake. She stiffened and pulled back.

Landon sighed. "Okay," he whispered. "I waited a whole year. Guess I can wait a little longer."

Chapter Ten

After three mugs of strong coffee, Kylie was still foggy. Last night had consisted of too much tossing and turning, and far too little sleep. Again. As if that weren't enough, the smell of her own baking was making her slightly nauseous.

The thing was, she'd been so disappointed when Landon had told her he wasn't sure about his future. The hurt had spread through her like wildfire as the realization that somewhere in the back of her mind, she'd wanted Landon to be the one. When had that happened? Since before she'd left Iowa, or since he'd walked back into her life?

There was a chance that he could end up quitting the rodeo in a year, build himself a fine ranch, and check all the boxes on her *list*. But that would mean taking a flyer on maybes.

On the other hand, he'd truly listened to her back in Iowa, understood what she'd needed and he'd waited a year before coming to find her. With the way she'd left, that was pure consideration. Just like Landon. He thought before he acted, considered the consequences, and not just for himself.

She remembered many times when he'd been there for her, whether it was helping her make dinner, or, more importantly, how he'd known to back off when she was confused or hurt by Gary. He'd been a real friend, and she'd taken advantage of his sincerity and kindness, even though she'd known he wanted more.

But what if she decided to explore what they had between them and ended up shattered? Again. It was possible. Maybe she was being too cynical, but would he have even bothered to seek her out if his broken leg hadn't kept him from competing?

Although, that didn't sound like the Landon she knew. Had known. Of course, she would never have imagined he'd become so cavalier about his plan.

So, she could take a risk, even with him not being certain about…things, and it might surpass her wildest dreams. Possible? Perhaps.

But she wouldn't know if she didn't try.

The mix of fear and excitement that swept through her at the thought was far more intense than anything she'd ever experienced before. Even starting The Cake Whisperer, which was still a pretty big deal for her. The only thing that would allow her to make this giant step was that it was for a short time. Two weeks. At the very least, at the end of it, she'd be wiser.

Of course, that would mean letting Landon know where she stood, which made the fear outweigh the excitement. At the ripe old age of twenty-six, she had literally no experience to fall back on. Gary had been it, and oh, that just made her want to weep.

The oven timer went off, and for a while, all she could concentrate on was getting the cakes to the cooling racks.

Kylie rubbed her throbbing temple and sighed.

Only nine-fifteen and she already needed to restock the display case. Evidently Landon was good for business. Folks in Blackfoot Falls loved their routine, yet customers who normally didn't come into the bakery on Thursdays had shown up the second she opened. Everyone had questions about him.

She'd played down their relationship, ignored the raised eyebrows, even as she imagined she could still feel the way his warm breath had brushed against her lips.

They'd almost kissed. But this time, it had been different. Maybe they should've gone for it, but no. She hadn't been ready last night.

"Hey, how about one of your specialty coffees to go?"

Landon's voice made her jump, and she bumped her hip hard against the counter.

"You scared the hell out of me," she muttered, rubbing her hip.

"The bell rang when I came in."

She took in his worn jeans and faded blue shirt, the sleeves rolled back, exposing his muscled forearms. He certainly looked like he was ready to get right to work.

"Why are you eyeing me like that?" he asked, laughing. "I didn't scare you on purpose."

"Where are your crutches?"

"Don't need them for this distance."

"Did you do your PT exercises?"

"Yes, ma'am. I'm a man of my word." He sounded chipper. It was awful.

Dragging her gaze away from him, Kylie wiped her hands on her apron. "You had a lot of physical activity yesterday. Don't feel as though you have to start right away. We haven't found you a helper yet."

"That's okay. I need to swing by the hardware store. Maybe the owner will know someone."

Kylie turned to get a tray of fritters she'd set on the back counter. "Oh, I should give you money."

"Nah, not yet. I'll keep the receipts. You left the garage open?"

"It's never locked. Another great thing about living here. I feel so safe."

Landon frowned. "Better not get overconfident. Even small towns have crime. And I heard you're having more tourists visiting town."

"That's true. Hopefully, that will also help my coffee bar business."

"You'll make it a success, Kylie. I have every faith in you."

The dark blue of his eyes tugged at her, drawing her into the place where logic disappeared. She almost wished the counter wasn't between them.

He glanced around, and said, "I really could go for a good shot of caffeine. Just skip all the frothy stuff."

"Well, you're welcome to the regular coffee, which I made on the strong side. But I'm not set up to make espresso or anything like that. Not until Joe finishes."

Landon gave her a patient smile. "How long have we known each other?"

"What does that— Four years. Why?"

"You think I don't know you? I bet you already have one of those fancy coffee stations. You ordered it a minute after you came up with the coffee bar idea."

"Are you implying I'm impulsive?"

"Nope. Enthusiastic." Amusement crinkled the corners of his eyes. "Am I right?"

Kylie sniffed. "I just got it yesterday. I haven't even had time to take it out of the box or read the instructions yet." She'd glanced at them, though, and the operating manual looked intimidating, probably because she was tired.

"Hey, I was just teasing."

"Smart-ass," she muttered under her breath.

Landon cut loose a surprised laugh.

"Oh, be quiet. The stupid instructions are longer than *War and Peace*. Try reading them with little sleep and a giant headache."

He cocked his left brow at her. "Trouble sleeping, huh? Any way I could be of service?"

She figured her glare was answer enough.

"Listen, I have some time," he said, just as someone opened the door. "Let me have a look at it."

Frowning slightly, Shirley entered with the binder of birthday cake photos she'd borrowed.

"Good morning," Kylie said.

The woman darted a look at Landon, who turned and nodded at her, before he stepped to the side.

"I came by yesterday afternoon but you'd closed early." She laid the binder on the counter, clearly annoyed.

"I apologize for that," Kylie said, and grabbed a to-go cup. "I put a sign out in the morning but next time I promise to give more notice." She poured the coffee and grabbed some cream. "Here you go, Shirley, on the house."

"Mornin'. We met the other day." Landon cranked up the charm. "I must say, you look mighty fetching today."

"Oh, for pity sake…" Fighting a smile, Shirley waved him off. To Kylie she said, "You look out for this one."

"Oh, I do. Believe me." Kylie met his eyes. The flutter in her chest made her turn abruptly to Shirley. "So, did you decide on a cake?"

"I have it narrowed down to two. They're all wonderful. You're very talented."

"That's what I keep telling her," Landon said as he came around the counter. "Excuse me, ladies. I'll get out of your way."

Kylie watched him continue into the kitchen. "Wait. Are you going to—"

"Yep."

"You don't know where—"

"I'll find it."

"Of course you will," Kylie muttered, rubbing her left temple.

Shirley stirred her coffee, but her gaze was on Kylie. "That young man sure is sweet on you."

Kylie felt her cheeks heat, and she eloquently said, "Uh…"

Shirley just smiled.

Kylie held her tongue, opened the binder and saw the two marked pages. "Ah, these cakes are both very popular, especially for large parties," she said, and went on to list the options.

Shirley listened, asked a few questions, and thankfully, dropped the subject of Landon.

If only Kylie could be so easily distracted. He wasn't making too much noise but she could hear him moving around in the kitchen and she had to force herself to concentrate on Shirley's order. Before they were squared away, Patty from the motel dashed in to pick up a box of cherry turnovers to take home.

After the women left, Kylie made her way into the kitchen. The espresso machine was set up on a small out-of-the-way section of the counter near the sink. On the floor was the box it had been shipped in, all the wrapping material stuffed neatly inside.

Landon's nose was buried in the manual, but he looked up the second he realized she'd joined him. "This is some contraption," he said, and returned to scanning the instructions. "It has a built-in grinder with five settings, an auto-cleaning and descaling feature…"

"I know."

"It makes espressos, cappuccinos, lattes...even plain ol' coffee."

"Uh-huh," she said, holding back a laugh.

He glanced up again. "Right. You know."

"I do. And I have the empty bank account to prove it."

"How much did this sucker set you back?"

Kylie sighed. "Too much."

"What? A grand?"

She cleared her throat.

"More?" he asked, his brows rising.

She picked up the carafe and put it in the sink. "This is low end. Some of them go for four thousand."

"That's crazy." He watched her reach for the dish detergent. "I already washed it."

"What?" She followed his gaze to the carafe. "You must really want that espresso."

"Nah." He set down the instructions. "I just figured I'd make myself useful—hey, how about I make you something? Feel daring?"

Her breath caught. Although his tone hadn't been the least bit suggestive, something in his eyes triggered a warm flush that spread through her body.

Oh, this was just plain silly. She'd better make a decision quickly.

"Maybe later," she said, switching her attention to the clock. "We'll end up getting interrupted." She swung her gaze back to him. "I mean, you know, before I can enjoy a cup in peace."

"Good point." He studied her closely, as if sensing the tension thrumming inside her. "You want me to move this?"

"It can stay there for now." She stared at the large espresso machine, thinking up something to say that would cut through the sudden awkwardness she felt. "Oh, and thanks for setting this up." When she finally risked looking up into his familiar face, a smile came easily. "It's been nice," she admitted, surprised when his brows lowered. "You know, having you around. It's nice."

Landon sighed. "You've gotta stop doing that, Kylie."

"Doing what?"

"Treating me like a brother."

"I just said it was nice having you around. How is that..." She trailed off, knowing he was probably right. "Old habit, I guess."

"Are you afraid you'll feel guilty if this thing between us turns out to be something?"

Unprepared for his directness, she hesitated. "I suppose it's possible, but I really don't know."

"You haven't been in contact with Gary, so I doubt that's the problem."

"Aren't you two still friends?"

"Not for a long time."

Her heart sank to her stomach. "Because of me?"

"I can't say that wasn't a factor," Landon said, with the candor she'd always admired. "But mostly it's the drinking. Every time he gets plastered, he whines about missing you and how the judging is rigged. His rodeo career is over. Everyone seems to know that but him."

Kylie sighed.

"Don't take that on yourself. He created the problem, not you."

"I know. I really do."

"I hope so." Landon caught her hand. "You went above and beyond catering to him. So much more than he deserved."

"You mean I was a doormat."

"No," he said, trying to tug her closer.

Kylie wouldn't budge. The lack of conviction she sensed in his response disappointed her. The truth would hurt but it was what she needed from Landon.

"Sometimes it appeared that way," he added slowly. "But I think something else was going on with you."

Startled and curious, she let down her guard. Another slight tug and she was close enough to feel his breath on her face. "What do you mean?" she asked, not at all sure she wanted to know the answer.

"I think you might've let Gary get away with so much because you felt guilty about being attracted to me."

She looked down, certain her cheeks were flaming. "We never crossed the line."

"Of course not. I'm not saying that. But refraining didn't keep *me* from feeling like crap."

His admission helped to calm her. She *had* felt guilty and angry and frustrated and so much more, all of which she'd thought she kept hidden, just to stave off arguments. But she'd learned a lot since then and no matter what happened, she wasn't ever going to be a doormat again.

He nudged her chin up. "You were never unfaithful."

Oh, but those shocking thoughts as she'd lain in bed each night… "You know what," she said, her face heating at the memories, "we've talked about Gary enough. Let's leave the past in the past. Yes, I felt something for you. That needs to be enough for now. And if that makes you feel as though you made the trip here for nothing, I'm sorry."

The bell announced a customer.

"Excuse me." Kylie nearly tripped in her haste to leave the kitchen.

A pair of Sundance guests who'd come by earlier in the week stood at the display case. "Hey, any chance you received that espresso machine yet?" The tall blonde dragged her gaze away from the chocolate cupcakes. "I'm seriously jonesing for a—"

Her gaze skipped past Kylie. Eyes widening, a smile lifted her lips.

The other woman looked up from the case with a gasp. "Landon Kincaid?"

Kylie already knew he'd walked out behind her. This wasn't the first time she'd seen the way women responded to him. But that these city women could so easily recognize him? Kylie had meant to look him up online last night, but she'd forgotten.

"In the flesh," he said. "You must be rodeo fans."

The blonde extended her hand. "I'm Bridget."

After wiping a palm on his jeans, he reached over the counter.

"I'm Leah and definitely a fan," the brunette said. "I saw you ride in Oklahoma the day you got hurt."

Landon winced. "Yeah, not my finest hour."

"All I could think was, poor baby." Leah seemed to be having trouble letting go of his hand. "You're still going to make it to the finals, right?"

With a slick move, he extricated himself and gave Leah a smile that was sure to smooth over any hurt feelings. "Count on it, darlin'."

Kylie tried not to roll her eyes. Or gag at how thick he was laying it on. It wasn't like him to be flirty, and it bothered her more than it should.

"Oh, good. I already have my tickets. I'll be sitting right up front."

"We both will," Bridget added. "What about tomorrow night? You're coming to the dance, right?"

Landon cocked a questioning brow at Kylie. "I don't know anything about it."

"They were late posting signs. But Rachel—she runs

the Sundance where we're staying." Bridget lowered her voice. "We're not from around here, but you've probably guessed that," she said with a flip of her blond hair, oblivious to Kylie standing right there. "Anyway, according to Rachel, it's really fun. Like an old-fashioned barn dance. Promise you'll come."

Quietly fuming, Kylie wondered how they'd like Pepto-Bismol lattes. She could make them look real pretty and taste like peppermint.

"And since I'm your number one fan," Leah said, "you should really save the first dance for me."

"Well, darlin' you seem to have forgotten. I'm still using crutches."

Bridget gave him a very purposeful smile. "Don't you worry, you can lean on me all you want."

Kylie had listened to all she could stomach. "Sorry, ladies, no special coffees available yet. May I get you something else?"

A loud horn sounded from outside.

Leah glanced back. "Damn, I forgot. It's Rachel. A group of us are going to Glacier National Park."

"She sure has been testy lately," Bridget said, sighing. "We better go."

The women started walking backward as if they couldn't bear to look away from Landon. "Tomorrow night," Leah said to him. "Don't forget."

"Or tonight…come next door to the Full Moon," Bridget added. "I'm buying." She opened the door but paused and frowned at Kylie. "Are you two brother and sister?"

"No," Kylie said, folding her arms across her chest.

Landon looked at her and grinned.

Rachel wouldn't let up on the horn so the two women scurried out the door.

"Guess I didn't make the trip for nothing after all," he said the second they were alone. "Huh, sis?"

Kylie unclenched her jaw. "I hate you right now," she muttered and headed into the kitchen, shutting out his laughter.

Chapter Eleven

Landon stood outside Kylie's garage, guzzling his third glass of ice water in as many minutes. Much as he hated working with the door open to prying eyes, the hot afternoon sun was kicking his ass.

Using the hem of his damp shirt, he blotted the sweat from his brow and squinted toward the snow-capped Rockies in the distance. Couldn't beat the view, and as for the heat, he'd be willing to bet this was unusual for September.

The neighborhood was made up of small, sturdy houses, probably built back in the 1920s, with their post-age stamp front yards and well-tended gardens. A few homes, like Kylie's, boasted white picket fences meant more for show than anything else.

All in all, it was a nice place. He could see how she would like it here, even though she was surrounded by much older neighbors. Hell, they were better than guard dogs. He liked knowing she had folks looking out for her.

Just as he was about to get back to work, he spotted a battered white pickup that reminded him of the old heap he'd gotten rid of three months ago. It had just turned off Main Street and was headed in his direction. Wouldn't surprise him if it was the kid Matt had found. The timing was right.

The driver slowed down, then pulled up behind Landon's truck in the driveway. The kid stuck his close-cropped dark head out the window and said, "Okay to park here?"

"Only if you're Barry."

Barry cut the engine and climbed out, eyeballing Landon's truck as he passed it. "Nice ride. Had it long?"

"A few months."

Landon shook his hand, glad the kid didn't appear to have anything to prove, although he wasn't sure who'd win in a fair fight. The kid had guns without being over-blown. Interesting, in this cowboy town, that he was into wrestling.

Landon walked with him into the garage, where Barry surveyed the equipment the way most riders weighed up horseflesh. Landon mentally debated how to bring up the subject of discretion. And that he had little experience using any of the equipment.

"Where did you get all these tools?" Barry asked, studying the big tricked-out worktable that would have even impressed Chad. "Matt?"

Landon nodded. "A few things are mine that I keep in the truck." Yeah, like the hammer and screwdrivers hanging off his new tool belt. The kid didn't need to know that.

Barry wandered over to the board Landon had set between two chairs. The one he'd been beating the tar out of. The chain he used to make dents in the ash was heavy as hell, but it was coming along pretty well, not to mention giving him a good upper body workout.

"Hot day to be distressing wood like this. You know I've done some of that using vinegar and steel wool. I could help."

"Thanks, but I'd rather you take over the actual construction." Landon noted Barry's confused frown, and just like that the perfect solution occurred to him. "Here's the thing, Kylie's worried I'll end up hurting my leg. I told her I'd be fine. But I can't take any chances. I gotta be able to get back on a horse soon."

"Rodeo, right?"

Landon nodded. "I got some plans you can look over, then we'll discuss what's in your wheelhouse. And how much you're charging."

Barry smiled. "I'm not dirt cheap, but only because I'm good."

"Yeah? I'll give you a chance to prove it. First, let me get us a couple of cold drinks and the plans. Then we can talk turkey."

The kid was cocky, but that was only a bad thing if he was trying to pull one over. Matt wouldn't have recommended the boy if he was full of it, but Landon would be careful. He wanted this project to go off without a hitch.

They ended up bartering back and forth, and when Barry finally agreed on a price, Landon decided to add a little incentive for the kid to keep his mouth shut. "Like I said, Kylie can't know you're doing most of the work or how much I'm paying you to do it. So, I'll give you a ten percent bonus if you keep everything about this project just between you and me. I mean no one else can know what we're doing, not even your girlfriend or your folks or Matt."

"Ten percent of the total?"

"Yep. And I'll set you up with some VIP tickets for the rodeo, how about that?"

Barry cleared his throat. "No offense, but would you care if I sold them? I'm starting college in January, and I'm trying to make sure my mom has some money put aside. Just in case."

"None taken."

They shook once more and Landon relaxed a notch. After hearing about Barry's experience and his take on the bench seat plans, Landon was hopeful that this would turn out to be a good deal for both of them.

The kid went back to his truck and settled his own fully loaded tool belt just under his waist. "So, you're ambidextrous?"

"What? No. Right-handed."

Barry gestured awkwardly toward Landon's belt. "It's, uh, more typical to put the most used tools near your dominant hand. I noticed on the shelf by the wall there was a chalk line, a carpenter's pencil and a hooked blade. Probably should keep those handy."

"Ah." Landon forced himself to meet Barry's eyes.

"You can use the left pockets for nails, screws, a chisel, that sort of stuff."

"Yeah, okay. Thanks."

Barry shrugged, and started working on the frame for the first base.

After setting up his belt, and deciding he'd never think of this experience again, ever, Landon went back to distressing the wood. Soon enough, they settled into an easy rhythm. The boy—actually, he was a young man—seemed certain of his moves, checked the plans several times, measured carefully.

It caught Landon by surprise when another truck pulled into the driveway. Turned out to be Joe, who must've been on his way to work at the bakery. Landon hoped Joe wasn't going to kick up a fuss about Barry.

"Well, damn," Joe said, taking his time checking out the setup. "I thought you'd be out here with a handsaw and some duct tape. Looks to me like you got yourself some good help—"

"Yeah, about that—"

"—which is fine by me." The older man took off his white cap and wiped his brow with the back of his hand. "I just got a job over in Twin Creeks that's gonna keep me hopping, what with the job at the bakery. But if you still need to use my workshop, we can work something out."

"Yeah, Barry's terrific. I got lucky. But if I need the workshop, I'll give you a call. It's more important for you to get Kylie's place ready, anyway."

"Sure thing." Joe nodded, apparently pleased.

"Good. Let me walk you out." Landon clapped Joe on the back, easing him out of the garage. Just as he hiked up into his truck, Landon leaned in. "Remember. Not a word to Kylie about any of this. Pretend we never talked, okay?"

Joe shook his head. "You think she knows you're sweet on her? Better you just tell her soon."

Landon sighed. First, a kid had to tell him how to wear a damn tool belt, and now Joe wanted to give him advice in the romance department. Riding a bucking bronc was much easier.

"Don't worry," Joe said. "I'll keep quiet."

As Landon watched him drive away, it occurred to him how much his success relied on a high school kid and a carpenter he barely knew to keep their mouths shut.

Good thing his brother had taught him to believe in miracles.

KYLIE LEFT THE Cake Whisperer in high spirits. She couldn't have been happier about Celeste starting at the bakery in two days. Not only had she come with glowing recommendations, Kylie really liked her. Plus, she wanted to work mostly mornings which were Kylie's busiest times.

A bonus was that Celeste was an excellent baker. In

order to stay home with her kids, she'd been supplementing the family's income by baking at home the same way Kylie had done back in Iowa. Celeste still had a small customer base but the business was too sporadic and she planned on directing them to The Cake Whisperer. Kylie insisted on giving her a commission for her delicious German sweet breads.

There was another reason Kylie was excited to have her start right away. If all went well, it was possible she'd have more time to spend with Landon. Not just to help him with the furniture, either. Just thinking about him and the decision she'd made speeded up her heart rate and her pace.

It was a beautiful day, and since the shop was closed and Joe was working she'd decided to take a dinner break at home. She'd walked the ten minutes from the bakery, as had become her habit while the good weather lasted.

As soon as she turned onto her street she could see his truck parked in her driveway. Someone in a white pickup was backing out and she hoped it was the boy Matt had found to help Landon.

Walking briskly past her neighbors' homes, she waved at the elderly couples sitting on rockers on their front porches. She'd met most of them the first day she'd moved in and figured they were keeping an eye on all the activity going on at her place.

Just before her driveway she heard a vehicle slowing behind her. The sheriff's truck stopped and the window went down.

Kylie sighed. "Hey, Grace. Don't tell me the neighbors called."

Grace laughed. "How long have you lived here now? Of course they did. Said a strange man was hanging around your house." Her gaze went toward the garage.

"Well, now I can see why everyone's up in arms. Need me to cuff him?"

Glancing back at Landon, Kylie grinned. "Would you?"

"I'm sure I could come up with a reason. Looks like a heartbreaker to me."

Kylie's smile faltered.

Landon spotted them, but he stayed where he was and nodded in acknowledgement.

"Well, crap," Grace said, frowning at Kylie. "Clearly I said something wrong. I'm sorry. For what it's worth, I don't know who he is. I haven't heard a peep from the rumor mill. I was just teasing."

"Don't worry about it. Really." It dawned on Kylie that Landon must be wondering what had prompted a visit from the sheriff, so she motioned him over.

He limped over, crutchless, sporting a well-placed tool belt on his slim hips, and smiled at Grace. "Howdy, Sheriff."

It took a second for Kylie to tear her gaze away from Landon's new look. "Grace, this is Landon. He's an old friend from—" Kylie stumbled over the last words. Well, he was a friend. What else could she say?

Grace didn't seem to notice. "Looks like she's got you working hard."

"She's a slave driver, all right."

Kylie rolled her eyes. "He's building some bench seats and tables for the bakery."

"Oh, that's a mistake," Grace said with a laugh.

"I won't make them too comfortable." Landon smiled, his gaze sweeping the row of houses across the street. "So, I'm guessing one of the neighbors called?"

"Three by my last count."

"They're a watchful bunch, but that's good for Kylie. I'm glad."

Grace seemed pleased with his remark. "It's a safe community. We had a poaching incident a couple years back when I first moved here, but that's it. Everything else has been petty misdemeanors, shoplifting or vandalism, drunk and disorderly, that sort of thing."

"Where did you move from?"

"Arizona. Came here for the job and I like it—most days. Anyway, I've got some work to do back in town. Some kids broke into the barn where the dance is being held and decided to get creative. My deputies just picked up the last one. They're going to be damn busy repainting all night." She looked at Landon. "You comin' to the dance?"

He looked at Kylie. "Are we?"

Grace chuckled and put the truck in gear. "Hope to see you tomorrow night," she said, as she eased her way down the street.

Landon moved closer. "And how was your day?"

"Good," Kylie said. "I'm much more interested in yours, though. Was that Barry I saw leaving in the white pickup?"

"Yep." Landon slowed as they got to the garage, with the door lowered most of the way. "No peeking," he said. "I want to make some headway before you see anything. And don't worry—Barry seems like he knows his stuff. He's already been a help today."

"But I want to help, too."

He turned to face her, both hands settling on her shoulders. "The whole point of this is to make your life easier. You worry about the coffee bar and Joe. I'll worry about the rest. Do we have a deal?"

"Not yet, we don't. First of all, how much help can Barry be if he's only able to come after school?"

"That's not going to be a problem. He's stretched out his senior year because he's been working a lot. Helping his single mom, I think. He only needs a few more credits to graduate and get the wrestling scholarship he's counting on. He's got every weekday and Saturday open to me."

Kylie sighed, and would have relaxed if not for the gentle squeezes to her shoulders. And how close the two of them were standing.

Landon had been working in the heat, and his hair was that messy side of sexy that could have easily come from a wicked night, and his shirt was unbuttoned enough for her to see a few dark hairs plastered to his chest. He smelled downright feral. It should have bothered her, the sweat, but instead it awakened something new inside her. As if she had a specific gene that had been made to respond to this musky scent, and she'd never known it until this moment.

"Okay?" he asked, bending so he could look straight into her eyes.

"Okay. I'm trusting you big-time here."

"I'm glad," he said, rising to his full height. "It's important to me that you can."

She smiled, hating that they were in full view of the neighbors. And hating that she hadn't counted on having to go back to the shop later. Maybe today wasn't the right time to say anything.

"So, how about dinner later?"

"Sorry. I can't," she said, not hiding her disappointment. "I'm just here to grab a quick sandwich, but you're welcome to join me. It was too disruptive at the shop after Joe started banging away, and so my new helper, Celeste, went home to feed her kids, but then she's coming back so we can go through the evening prep together. I have no idea how long it's going to take."

His hands dropped to his sides, which disappointed her, but then she realized she could see inside the garage. At least a little bit. Not nearly enough to figure out what he'd been up to all day.

"Hey. I said no peeking." His stern look had her holding back a grin. "Am I going to have to move in here just to keep an eye on you?"

She could feel her cheeks heat. The idea of him staying with her was something she'd already thought about. "Right," she said. "I apologize, but I really didn't see anything. And I do need to get back to the bakery soon, so…sandwich? I have only tuna and cold cuts. And there should be some beer left, unless you guys wiped me out."

"I'll take you up on that drink, but I'm too gross to eat now."

"Gross? Not to me. I kind of like carpenter Landon."

He blinked at her, offering up a little smile as he moved a bit closer. "Well, then. I guess I'll take you up on that sandwich."

"Good," she said, standing there like an idiot, wondering if she'd said too much or not enough. "Guess I need to go in through the front door. Meet me in the kitchen after you wash up…"

The sentence fell away as an image flashed in her mind—him walking out of her bathroom wearing only a towel, a few drops of water easing down his chest…

"Kylie?"

"Tuna or bologna?"

"Tuna sounds great."

"Tuna it is," she said, inwardly sighing at her sparkling banter. As she let herself in the front door, she thought again about his suggestion. He'd been teasing, but in the middle of the afternoon she'd decided to ask him. At some point. The guest room, though, to start. As she scurried to get the sandwiches made, she heard him come in through the garage door, then she heard the one to the bathroom closing. It was a small house.

Which made the idea of sharing it with him completely crazy. But if she was going to jump in, it might as well be into the deep end. Or at least not the wading pool. Further confirming how insane she'd been, she was halfway to the bathroom with his beer before she spun on her heel and raced back to the kitchen to finish their dinners.

A few minutes later, she sensed him behind her and she turned her head.

His hair was damp, combed back, and he was removing his tool belt. "Sorry," he said, "I should've left this in the garage."

She briefly thought about asking him to leave it on. How ridiculous was that? "No problem. Just…leave it anywhere."

He stashed it somewhere around the corner, then pulled out a chair for her at the small kitchen table.

She brought their plates and their drinks with her, and sat down. "You know what you said about you staying at the house? That's not a bad idea."

His eyebrows rose and his smile grew.

"I've only got the one bathroom, so we'd have to share, but that shouldn't be too much of a problem. I mean, why pay for the motel when you can use my spare room?"

His smile drooped, as did his brows.

She held back a grin, wondering if he knew how transparent—and impatient—he looked. "You wouldn't need to eat out," she said, going over the list she'd come up with earlier as she was helping customers. "And you'd be able to take breaks during the day. You know, to rest your leg. I mean, I know you do that now, but you'd have the option of getting horizontal." She licked her dry lips. "Okay, that came out weird but I think you get it."

"Yep. All sound reasons," he said. "A very excellent idea. The spare room would be real...convenient."

Although now that she'd gotten it all out and he'd accepted her offer, she felt herself flush. She had no idea what to say next. Earlier she'd been so excited that she hadn't once considered how awkward this could become. Once he moved in—oh, they hadn't discussed when...

He put down his sandwich. "You know, you can still change your mind."

Realizing how closely he'd been studying her, she blinked. "I won't."

"Tell you what, take some time. Think about it overnight."

"I don't—" She nodded. "You, too. You can still change your mind."

"Not gonna happen," he said.

"Me, neither." She took a sip of water, scared but excited. Him. Her. Holy cow!

"Okay, but I won't check out until we touch base in the morning. Just in case."

She smiled. He wasn't the only one who was impatient.

Chapter Twelve

The next morning, Kylie called while Landon was in the shower. After cursing that he'd missed her, he quickly opened the text she'd left.

Bring apples on your way home, please. And your things.

Landon, having already packed, pumped his fist. He'd dreamed about Kylie all night, and in his fantasies he sure hadn't been sleeping in the guest room.

Leaving his bag for the moment, he went down to the lobby and poured himself a cup of coffee. Several other guests were indulging in the muffins he recognized as Kylie's handiwork. Instead, he grabbed an apple, figuring he'd supplement it with something more substantial later. Even though his physical therapy got him sweating, as did distressing the wood, it wasn't even close to what he normally did. Now, more than ever, he needed to stay in shape. Once he returned to the circuit, every ride would count if he was going to make it to the finals.

Patty was behind the front desk, helping someone, so he stood a respectful distance away and sipped his coffee as he waited to let her know he'd be checking out. Naturally, his thoughts went to Kylie. Her day had started several hours ago, but he had a clear mental picture of what she looked like when she woke up in the morning. Back in the day her tousled hair and sleepy eyes had always made him smile. She'd never been much of a morning person. He wondered if having the bakery had changed that.

He'd find out soon enough.

The man at the front desk took his credit card receipt, picked up his bag and turned for the door. Landon was about to step up when Kevin entered the lobby. For a small-town motel manager, he looked overdressed in a crisp white shirt, navy blue blazer and gray dress slacks.

Kevin said good morning to Patty before he spotted Landon...who froze in his tracks. He was such an idiot. How in the hell had he not considered how his moving out of the motel would affect Kylie? Gossip was a popular small-town hobby. People would see him around and guess he was staying with her.

"Still here, huh?" Kevin said, all friendly and showing a lot of teeth.

Yeah, who was he kidding? The guy must've been checking the guest log twice a day, hoping Landon had split. Patty's lowered gaze and struggle to squash a smile confirmed it.

"Yep," Landon said, forcing himself to relax, when he really wanted to kick himself three ways to Sunday. "You have a nice town here."

"It's grown on me," Kevin said, sizing him up and frowning. "Did you get a job or something?"

Landon looked down at his scuffed boots and worn, ripped jeans. His brown T-shirt had seen better days too. "I'm just doing some carpentry work for Kylie."

"I thought she already had someone."

"Yeah, Joe Hopkins. He's working in the bakery. I'm building the seats and tables." Landon glanced at the wall clock behind the desk. "I need to get moving. Got a lot of work ahead of me today."

"Sure." Kevin nodded, clearly distracted. "Any idea when you're leaving?"

"Not yet." He made a quick decision. "Look, if you need to adjust my room rate I totally understand. You didn't know I'd be here this long when you gave me the discount. I don't want you getting in trouble with your boss."

Kevin snorted. "I am the boss. We'll keep you at the same rate," he said, irritation beginning to show in the tightening of his mouth. "Since you're a friend of Kylie's."

"Okay. Thanks. I appreciate it."

"Hey, I appreciate you helping her out," Kevin said. "Wish I had the time to do it myself."

Landon didn't miss the proprietary message. No one who was listening could. He just smiled and went to get a coffee refill to take upstairs with him.

He'd keep the room and leave a few of his clothes behind, trade them out every other day, mess with the bed, just so it looked like he was using the room. As far as anyone knew, he was still at the motel and not staying with Kylie. It wasn't just about the rumors. He didn't want to mess anything up for her. Including Kevin. Landon wasn't happy about it, but he wanted her to be with him by choice, not process of elimination. And yeah, he'd stay in that spare room as long as she wanted him to, but he couldn't help hoping the situation would change quickly.

LANDON SPOTTED BARRY'S truck in front of Kylie's place as soon as he turned the corner. Good for him. It was 8:45 a.m. and Barry had committed to coming in by nine for the next five days.

As Landon parked, he was even more impressed when

he saw that Barry was stacking the long sheets of untreated ash that were for the bench seats. The miter saw was set up, ready to go. The kid didn't stop, just gave a quick nod before finishing the stack and putting one sheet on the worktable.

"What time did you get here?" Landon asked, walking his crutches to the far left corner before he put on his tool belt.

"About eight-thirty. I can't do that all the time, but this morning my mom chased me out of the house. She wants me to make a good impression."

"It's working. You have brothers? Sisters?"

"Yep. A brother and sister, both younger. Which makes it hard for my mom to work full-time."

"What about your dad?"

Barry kept his eyes on the worktable. "He left. Which was a good thing. He was a mean drunk and allergic to work."

"I'm sorry. My father died when I was seventeen, and that was hard enough. It must have put a lot of pressure on you, being the oldest. I know I've always counted on my two older brothers."

Barry shrugged. "It's not that bad. I just want to do as much as I can before I leave."

"I never asked which school you're going to."

"Oklahoma State."

"Good for you. I'm glad I went to college, even though I left after two years to rodeo. Although I'm kinda sorry I didn't major in something more useful than history."

Barry turned his head, not quick enough to stop his laugh. But that was okay. Landon had heard it all. "What about you?"

"Business. And a minor in farm and ranch management."

"That's great. You can do a lot with that, and live and work anywhere in the country."

"That's my goal. But first I have to make sure I can keep my scholarship."

"I'm sure your mom's real proud of you."

Barry ran his hand over the piece of wood on the table. "She's not always been all that healthy," he said. "But she still works hard."

Landon wrapped the distressing chain a little too tightly around his fist. He thought about his own family, how they'd all supported each other through some tough times, especially after his dad's passing. The idea of a father running off was unimaginable.

He got started on bashing the wood up. Last night, he'd looked up that vinegar and steel wool method. He was considering trying that on the tables, since it would make the ash look aged, but keep the surface smooth. Although using the chain was giving him a needed workout.

The sound of the saw combined with the chain slamming into the wood almost made him miss his cell phone ringing in his pocket. He was pretty winded as he walked out of the garage. It was Kylie. He couldn't have stopped his smile if he'd tried.

"Hi," she said. "I left a six-pack and some sandwich stuff in the fridge. There's a fresh loaf of bread on the counter, and some cookies in the big bear jar. Did you remember the apples?"

"Yes, and when did you have time to do all that?"

"I managed," she said, but then he heard her voice, muffled, saying something about a cake. "Sorry." Her voice was back to normal. "We've got three birthday cakes to finish this morning, and Celeste is still learning how to decorate, so that's all on me."

"Does that mean you're going to be late tonight?"

"Does that mean you're going to be there when I get off?"

He bit off a chuckle. "Damn," he said. "I certainly hope so."

She was quiet for a little too long, making him wish he hadn't been such a smart-ass.

"Landon Kincaid. That's not a nice thing to do when I'm at work."

"What? I just meant—"

"I know exactly what you meant."

After clearing his throat, he said, "My bag's in the truck. I didn't want to bring it in yet. Barry was here when I arrived. The kid's a hard worker."

"That's great."

"Yeah," he said, turning away from a nosy neighbor across the street. "Also, I wanted to make sure you hadn't changed your mind."

The only response was silence, and his heart nearly stopped.

"Sorry," she said, and he was relieved to hear customers yapping in the background. She'd been distracted, that was all. "Didn't you get my text? I figured you'd know it was safe to check out."

He almost said something about what had occurred to him earlier, but thought better of it. She'd just worry about the gossip even though he'd, in effect, taken care of that. And she had enough on her mind. "Yep, I got it. Just double-checking. Barry leaves at three. I'll get settled into the spare room after. Hope the bed's not a single. My feet always stick out the end."

"It may not be motel grade, but I think you'll fit just fine," she said, her voice a little huskier than it was a minute ago.

"Yeah?"

"Three birthday cakes. I need to go. I should be home at around four. After, we can talk about checking out the dance."

"You bet. Anything I can do to help before you get here?"

"Yeah. Don't make a mess. I'll see you later."

She was gone before he could say goodbye. As he put his phone away, he thought about what it would be like to have a normal evening alone with Kylie, eat dinner, maybe watch some TV, make out on the couch like kids. The only word that came to mind was *sweet*.

KYLIE WAS A bundle of nerves as she opened her front door. She had no business being anything but confident. She'd decided on a game plan. They could go by the dance, just to socialize. And when they got back? She'd be the one to initiate the first kiss. That should surprise the heck out of Landon. The thought of being in his arms made her shivery with anticipation.

He was nowhere in sight, but she could see that the door to his room was open. "Landon?"

"Hey," he said, although she still didn't see him. Then he walked out of his room, shirtless, hair damp, jeans on, barefoot.

She needed to sit down.

"I took advantage of your shower."

"Good water pressure, huh?" She clenched her teeth. *Good water pressure?*

The right side of his mouth curled up. "I agree. Heats up fast, too."

"Okay. That was stupid," she muttered. "Feel free to go finish dressing. I didn't mean to disturb you."

He didn't move. Well, nothing besides his eyes as they swept down her body. She wasn't wearing anything special. Work khakis and a T-shirt, something she didn't mind getting messed up at the shop. Her hair must have been a sight though, and she hadn't even thought about checking it before she'd walked home.

While he, on the other hand, looked…beyond perfect.

"I wasn't sure what to wear," he said. "I mean, if you still wanted to go to the dance. Or go out to dinner first?"

"I don't know. Do you have a preference?"

The look he gave her made her weak in the knees. She bet if she looked up *smoldering* in the dictionary, she'd see a picture of his darkened eyes.

"I want to do whatever you want," he said. "I'm easy that way." He took a step toward her. "As long as I'm with you, I'm happy watching the grass grow."

She smoothed her hair and moved around him into the kitchen. She'd been home all of ten seconds and already she was rethinking her master plan. "I defrosted a casserole before I left this morning. I'll just put it in the oven and it'll be ready in forty minutes. I'll take a shower while it's heating. I can make a salad, too."

Now that there was some distance, she turned to face him. His smile was still in place, a bit sadder maybe. She should have kissed him.

No. Kissing was for after. And even though she wanted him so badly, there was time, right? Despite the fact that she had to force herself not to touch his tanned chest, run her hands over every last muscle.

"Whatever you want is fine with me."

"Do you even like chicken and noodle casserole?"

"Love it."

She exhaled, frustrated at her inability to be the least bit cool. She wasn't a teenager, even though she was acting like one. "Hey, I meant to ask," she said, grasping for a change of subject. "Do you have the invoices for the stuff we've bought so far? I was just wondering where we're at."

He blinked a couple of times. Maybe the change of topic was a bit too abrupt. "I have everything, but I haven't put it all together. Don't worry, though, you're still within your budget."

"Oh, good," she said, opening the fridge. She put the casserole on the counter, and when she turned to put the oven on, Landon was so close she nearly stepped on his bare foot. "Oh!"

"Hello, Kylie. How was your day? Did you get all three birthday cakes finished in time?"

She let out a soft laugh. "Hello, yourself. Yes, thank you. The cakes were big hits. Joe showed up on time. Celeste is doing a great job. And how was your day?"

"Frankly, the best part of it is right now." He leaned toward her but kept his hands at his sides.

Without even realizing it, she found her hand frozen partway to his chest.

He took a small step closer. Though not quite to the point of touching. That would be up to her.

"Whatever you want," he whispered.

Oh, screw it. She couldn't stop herself from that one final step. This was Landon. The man she'd never been able to stop thinking about. And she'd waited too long already.

Her hands landed on his chest, just above his heart, and she felt his muscles tense. She moved her head closer to his neck, wanting to scent him like a wild creature. As she inhaled, the flesh beneath her hand quivered, and she jerked up, almost hitting his jaw before she tried to step back. "Oh."

"Don't," he whispered, his big hand coming up and

touching her gently under her chin with one finger. That's all. Just one.

"You smell nice," she whispered.

"So do you. Like sugar and spice."

"I should probably shower." They were looking into each other's eyes, again, and she had no desire to move.

"Not from where I'm standing. I wasn't being poetic. You really do smell like the best dessert a man could ever have," he said, his gaze unwavering. "I can almost taste…"

Her breath left her, but her courage only strengthened. "Yes?"

His smile was as warm as the hand that curled behind her neck. Slow as molasses he lowered his head, and when they were close enough that she could feel his heat, smell the fresh scent of the man beneath the soap, she made her move.

He grunted a little bit, probably with surprise, and then he was kissing her back.

Soft. Careful.

Wanting more, she increased the pressure.

His moan filled her mouth, then he wasn't so gentle. He pressed against her, trapping her hand so that she could feel his heart beating rapidly, matching the rhythm of her own.

Her lips parted just enough for him to slip his tongue inside quick as a wink. But he took his time once he was there. Slowly tasting, teasing, exploring. His fingers were running up the back of her neck into her hair, and she had goose bumps to match her shivers.

Her own moan snuck out, and she felt his lips curve up. That was a sweet extra.

Had she ever been this swoony over a kiss? Not that she could recollect. It was even better than she'd imagined. Standing was becoming difficult, as his every move made her tremble.

When he pulled back, it wasn't far.

"The spare room bed is all made up," she said. "It's a long single."

"I noticed."

"Mine's a queen."

He stilled. Even his chest. His breathing.

"Join me?" she whispered, hardly believing the words were hers, but sure. So sure.

"You sure?"

She smiled. "Yes."

"You know how long I've been waiting for this?" he said, leaning back so he could meet her gaze.

"How long?"

"Forever."

LANDON WOKE UP to the early light of dawn sneaking through the curtains in Kylie's bedroom, but all he cared about was the woman sleeping next to him. Her hand was lying on his chest, her head tucked into the curve of his neck. It felt like winning the world champion title. Like he'd arrived after a year-long journey straight into his fondest dream.

Landon had wanted her from the start. Not that he hadn't tried to do the decent thing and forget about her. But the pull had been too great. She was his ideal woman— her kindness, her sense of humor, the way she looked, and on a deeper level, he knew they shared the important things, like home and loyalty, and wanting a family. He'd even understood her trying so hard with Gary, despite the bastard's behavior toward the end. She was a woman who didn't run away from life's brutal pitfalls.

He didn't want to wake her, but he couldn't hold back from brushing a wisp of hair off her cheek.

Last night, she'd been a little shy, a little daring. He'd gotten a little overexcited, but they'd just laughed. Being with her like that was something he'd never forget, no matter what the future held.

"You're awake," he whispered when he saw her lashes flutter. "I hoped you would sleep a bit longer. I kept you up past your bedtime."

She blushed a pretty pink. "What time is it?"

"Time for a kiss," he said, pulling her up against his chest, the feel of her hard nipples driving him crazy.

"Wait," she said, her voice a breathless whisper.

"For...?" He kissed her neck, right where he knew she liked it, and inhaled her sweet womanly scent. After a long passionate night, how could he want her this desperately?

If Landon had his way, he would call Barry and tell him to take the day off. Hell, he'd like to call the whole town and tell them to get their donuts and birthday cakes somewhere else, then he and Kylie could spend the day in bed.

She pulled back. Not a lot, just enough so they could look at each other.

"Last night was wonderful," she said, her beautiful eyes meeting his. "You were wonderful."

"I knew it would be like this," he said. "No, that's not true. I couldn't have imagined it would be this..."

She sighed, then suddenly her face paled and her eyes widened. "What time is it?"

"About six."

"No, no, no, how could I have slept through the alarm? I've left Celeste to do everything by herself." She was scrambling, pulling the blankets up to cover herself, fighting the sheets with her feet. "I've got to go."

"Yes. Okay. Just, before you leave, let me kiss you."

She stilled. "Yes." Right before their lips met, she murmured, "Oh God, I'm going to be so late."

Chapter Thirteen

Mrs. Ramsey's dahlias were still in bloom, and Kylie slowed her step to take in the beautiful colors. Pinks, reds, purples, and especially the blue flowers were thriving. Behind them were a row of gladiolas, yellow and white and peach, a perfect backdrop for the drama of the dahlias. It was a real treat to see them this late in the season. After the first frost, they'd be gone.

She continued down her street, aware of the lightness of her step, and how stupidly happy she was. It was nice, just for a few minutes, to let herself bask in the feelings. Yes, there were reasons to put the brakes on her giddy heart—there was still so much she wasn't sure about. But Landon had only been staying with her for five days, so she supposed it was okay for her to feel as if she'd won the lottery.

The only thing she had to keep in mind was that this wasn't necessarily the beginning of something bigger. Although, it could be, and that's where the risk was, wasn't it? Landon would be returning to his own life soon. And at the rate he was healing, it might be sooner than either of them had anticipated. She'd be busy with the bakery and he'd be busy winning rodeos and…so much could happen. Still, worrying about that served no purpose now.

Things were going great with Celeste, who was a quick

learner with a good eye and talent that would only grow as she decorated more cakes. The customers liked her, and she'd even taken the time to figure out the espresso machine, then walked Kylie through the process until they were both comfortable.

If only Joe had been working as hard as Celeste and Landon. She understood the man had another job, but that shouldn't interfere with hers. After all, she'd hired him first. As it was, he sometimes showed up late and he'd missed two full days, when the whole job was supposed to have taken one week.

On the other hand, according to Landon, the tables and the bench seats were almost done. Happily, the warm weather had helped the varnish dry on all the wood, and Barry was a big help. A nice kid, too. She'd had lunch at home twice with the two of them.

As Kylie neared the house she made up her mind to ask Joe to work over the weekend to make up for his lost time. In fact, she'd insist. After all, the counter should have been finished by now.

It hadn't helped matters that she'd been getting less sleep than she needed. Having Landon in her bed was far too much of a temptation. He honestly had to be the sexiest man alive.

He was also adventurous enough to make her blush even now, and he'd never once just rolled over and went to sleep, leaving her hanging.

Ugh, no, she wasn't going to ruin things by thinking of the past. Living in the moment was working for her big-time. Plenty of life ahead for regrets. But being with Landon wouldn't be one of them.

The garage door was shut when she reached her house, both trucks parked outside. She wouldn't bother them.

After a sad look at her plain grass lawn, she couldn't help taking a moment to imagine what it could be.

She didn't linger, though, since she wanted to make lunch and surprise the guys.

After dropping her purse on the end table, she heard voices on her way to the kitchen. The door to the garage stood open. The temptation to peek was enormous, but she'd given her word. Though she hadn't made any promises about not listening.

"...great stuff."

Landon's voice. Just hearing it made the butterflies in her stomach flutter.

"Seriously. We're further ahead than I expected. You sure you want to major in business instead of working in carpentry? You'd do well."

"Nah," Barry said. "I need to be able to count on a steady income."

"It's a risk, that's true."

For a moment, the sound of what Kylie guessed was an electric sander drowned out everything. If she were a better person, she'd shut the door and get busy making meatloaf sandwiches. But she'd never claimed to be a saint.

"So, if you didn't have to worry about your siblings or your mom working so hard, what would you do?"

There was silence for a moment, then more sanding or whatever, then quiet again.

"It doesn't matter."

"Maybe not," Landon said.

She could hear him walking with one crutch. They'd gotten carried away last night, and when she'd asked if he was okay, he'd said yes. Liar. At least he was being careful today.

"You know how I told you about my dad dying," Landon said. "It was my senior year, and out of the blue he had a massive heart attack. He'd been healthy, active. Anyway, I'd been breaking mustangs since I was about fourteen and Dad and my brothers noticed I had a talent for it, and they encouraged me.

"After the grieving, and man, that went on for a long time, I figured my rodeo dreams were over. I felt real guilty for being pissed about that. I was even angry—" Landon cleared his throat. "I was angry at him for dying. It was my brothers who yanked me out of my funk. I was sure I had to work extra hard on the ranch to make up for my dad, but they kept pushing me to keep going. Insisted our dad would have wanted me to do what I loved. They swore they had the ranch covered."

After a short silence, Barry asked, "Did you leave right away?"

"I didn't completely believe them, but I was seventeen and I wanted to rodeo more than I wanted air. So after high school, I enrolled at a local college. I figured I could help at home and still manage to rodeo on the weekends if the events were close enough. It turned out to be too much so I quit school."

Seconds ticked by without either of them speaking.

"Probably a good choice," Barry said finally. "I mean, you know, a degree in history…"

Landon laughed. "Shut up, smart-ass. And pass me that Phillips."

Kylie smiled, picturing his slightly flushed face as Barry laughed along with him. She was about to back away when the pounding stopped and Barry said, "You went pro about eight years ago, right?"

"About that. I told myself I'd win a bunch of money and pay for some of the expenses at the ranch, ease the burden that way. Did okay, too. I was no wunderkind, but I was moving up the ranks."

"Yeah, but then you were like...gone for a while."

"Hey, you been researching me, kid?"

"Well, yeah," Barry said. "Gotta get a fix on the boss, you know?"

"Hell, when I was your age—"

"Oh, man, here we go."

Landon chuckled.

"And by the way," Barry said, "you're only ten years older than me."

"Ten years older, and don't forget wiser."

"I'm not the one with the broken leg," Barry mumbled, and Kylie had to cover her mouth to keep from laughing out loud. "You don't have to tell me why you dropped out of rodeo."

"Nah, it's fine. My oldest brother had an accident at the ranch, so I went home to help out. When things got back to an even keel, I had to think long and hard about what to do, but I decided to ride again. I've got no regrets about that. Most days, anyway."

This time when they quieted, Kylie ordered herself to go to the kitchen but her feet couldn't seem to move.

"Well, I'm glad it worked out for you," Barry said, his voice serious and gruffer than before. "But I'm the oldest son."

"Does your mom ever talk to you about your future? What she expects of you?"

"She wants me to be happy. That's all she ever says. But Julie and Ned are teenagers now. They'll need more things for school, clothes and stuff."

"Sounds to me like they're about ready to get jobs themselves."

"No way. That's the whole point."

"Listen, Barry. I'm not telling you to change your goals, to work any less, do anything different. But you know how you feel about helping your family? That sense of satisfaction that sits deep and low? And how even when it's a pain, there's still pride in every extra job you take on?"

Sanding again. Then, "Yeah."

"Don't you want Julie and Ned to feel that? To know they stepped up? That they helped so that you could take advantage of the things you've earned, like that scholarship. College?"

Kylie sniffled. But only because she'd been smelling all those flowers. Things got real quiet in the garage, and when she heard Landon's one-crutch walk, she scurried like a mouse into the living room, grabbed her purse, and walked into the kitchen, innocent as the day she was born.

"Hey, you just get here?" Landon asked, his smile warming her better than the sun.

"Thought I'd make you two some lunch. Hungry?"

"Yeah. I'd meant to put something together a while ago, then I got sidetracked."

"How's your leg?"

"Good." He leaned the crutch against the wall. "I'm just taking precautions, like I promised."

Guilt shot through her, but she hadn't peeked, so technically, Kylie was still in the clear.

"Tell you what. I'll knock on the door when lunch is ready, how's that?"

"What, no kiss first?"

Kylie glanced toward the garage door.

"He won't see us," Landon said, moving closer. "And if he did, would that be so bad?"

"Does he know you're staying here?"

"I doubt he's given it a single thought." He put his

arms around her and pulled her against him. "But I didn't say anything."

She lifted her chin, getting tingly just knowing his lips were about to touch hers. Lowering his head he gave her a quick kiss. Way too quick. She was about to complain, then felt his mouth skim the side of her neck, leaving a damp trail to her ear. He caught her earlobe between his teeth and gave a slight tug, before returning to slip his tongue between her lips.

Kylie shivered down to the soles of her feet.

"You're nervous," he said, leaning back. "Because of Barry?" Landon lowered his arms.

"No, that's not it. If I'm worried at all it's because I'm afraid I'll get carried away."

"Oh, well in that case..."

Kylie laughed, swatting his hands away when he tried to take hold of her. "Go. Wash up. I have to hurry if I want to eat with you guys."

"Sure, tease me like that, then push me away. Don't worry about my hurt feelings."

"You should be more concerned about that," she said, glancing at the bulging front of his jeans. "Wash up first, then get Barry."

Landon looked down. "He's seen this condition before, I promise."

"Oh, I can't hear this." She laughed as she turned to the fridge, knowing her cheeks were pink.

"To be continued." Landon kissed the nape of her neck, then jumped back to avoid a swat. "See you in five?"

"Make it ten." She got busy, knowing this was going to make her later than what she'd told Celeste, but not sorry she'd stopped to listen.

She hadn't known some of that stuff about Landon's

dad and his family. He'd told her his father had died, and only recently about his brother's accident having been the family emergency. She'd even known about him breaking mustangs as a teenager. But his brothers encouraging him to return to the circuit, his guilt over it…that he'd never mentioned.

While they had talked about personal things, she sure hadn't shared anything about her mother. As it was, she feared Landon knew more about Darlene than Kylie cared to acknowledge.

Mostly though, she was impressed with how he'd opened himself up to a kid he'd barely known a week. Barry was self-effacing, quiet, but he couldn't hide the fact that he thought he was pretty awesome at wrestling and carpentry. Nothing wrong with believing in yourself. If she hadn't, she wouldn't have The Cake Whisperer right now. But Landon had seen deeper and reached out.

It didn't take long to finish making their lunches, and both men washed their hands before they sat down. She didn't have much to say about her day, so she mostly listened to the two of them. Barry asked about breaking mustangs, and Landon was all too happy to fill him in on what it was like and how much he loved it.

Then Barry started bragging about his wrestling injuries, and added a couple from construction mishaps.

She just ate and smiled. Grateful for the day, grateful that she liked a man who could share himself with someone in need. Someone who, despite his big muscles and skillful hands, was just a kid trying to fill shoes far bigger than the ones his father had left behind.

Leaving Landon to clean up the kitchen, she hurried back to work. During a lull in customers, she confronted Joe, listened to him complain for about fifteen minutes, then made sure he would make up for his lost time. Finally, though, she hung out the Closed sign, and while she was more than ready to go home, she had a stop to make, first.

Kevin was in his office at the motel, as she knew he'd be, and the way he lit up when he saw her made her stomach tighten. But not being honest with him would be worse. She'd already begged off on a second date.

"What brings you here?" he asked, rounding his desk. He put his hand on her back and kissed her cheek, before he held the visitor's chair out for her.

Once they were both sitting, she took a deep breath. "I wanted to let you know that something's changed."

"Oh?"

"It's about my friend Landon." She looked away, then forced herself to meet Kevin's gaze. "We were strictly friends back in Iowa but…"

He started nodding as if this wasn't new information. "Now it's more."

"Yes. And I honestly have no idea what's going to come of it."

Kevin looked at her somberly. "I like you, Kylie. A great deal. But I don't want to make a fool of myself. Any more than I already have."

"You haven't. You've been nothing but great. And I'm being as honest as I can."

"I appreciate that."

She stood, and he did as well, but before he could come around the desk, she went to the door. "Thanks for being so understanding."

He just looked down and didn't respond.

AFTER CROSSING THE STREET, she saw Landon's truck coming down the block. The moment he stopped, she climbed into the passenger side and before she could get a word out, he pulled her straight into a kiss.

When they finally took a breath, Landon relaxed in his seat. "I've been thinking about that all day."

"I imagine you had a few other things on your mind."

"A few. But we could get arrested for those."

Grinning, she buckled her seat belt. "Yeah, let's not do that."

"You sure? Might've been a slow day. Could give Grace something to do."

She picked his hand up off her thigh and put it on the wheel. "Drive."

"Yes, ma'am," he said, putting the truck in gear. "Where to? Feel like going out to dinner?"

"Nope. Let's stay home."

"Works for me."

"Oh. I almost forgot. Rachel and Matt have invited us to dinner at their place tomorrow night."

"That sounds good." He checked the rearview mirror then pulled away from the curb. "I told you about him stopping by the other day?"

"Yes. And I'm sure it wasn't because he was worried you'd ruined his worktable."

"Maybe just a little." His mouth curved in that lop-sided smile she loved so much. "Tomorrow I'll pick up a nice bottle of wine."

"Uh, maybe we should get them something Rachel can enjoy also?"

"Well, that eliminates chocolates. Flowers?"

"That's perfect."

"I'm still getting a bottle of wine, though."

Wondering about her decision not to mention her visit with Kevin, Kylie sighed.

Landon glanced at her. "Is that a no on the wine?"

"What? No. I mean, yes. Wine would be great. In fact, get two bottles. Trace and Nikki will be there, and probably another couple. Also, I've been thinking about my neighbor's flowers."

"Okay," he said with a laugh. "What, you want me to go steal them for Rachel?"

"Ha. Funny. Anyway, the white house with the green shutters? Do you know the one I'm talking about?"

"Vaguely."

"You really can't miss all the dahlias and gladiolas growing along the porch. They're absolutely stunning, but I was surprised anything would still be blooming this far north."

"Not for much longer, though."

"Still, it gives me hope for my own garden. I can't wait till next summer to plant some flowers and vegetables. There's room for a small greenhouse in the backyard, too, and I want to grow dwarf fruit trees and lots and lots of berries."

"Don't you rent the house?"

She nodded. "But I think the owner might be willing to go for a rent-to-own deal. The place is perfect for me. It's close to work, and it's big enough for me to have people over. I really miss having homegrown veggies and fresh blooms for the table."

Landon was silent while they waited for some teenagers to cross the street. Kylie wondered if she should've been more diplomatic. But it had only been a week and they hadn't spoken about the future, and if anything, he should be relieved that she wasn't expecting a commitment. Still, she wished she'd thought first.

He looked at her and smiled. "Barry's turned out to be a hell of a helper. He's really good, and without him, no way I'd be this close to finishing."

"So you've said." Three times so far, not that she would bring that up.

Instead of turning onto her street, Landon went around the block, then drove down the only other residential street off Main. "I was thinking, since Celeste is doing so well and Joe's working over the weekend, and Barry's finishing up the bench seats, how about going with me to see my family?"

"What?" She stared at him. He looked serious. "For how long?"

"It's only six hours away. We can leave Friday after you close. Drive back Sunday night. Or Monday morning if you think Celeste can handle things."

Kylie didn't know what on earth to say. Sunday was the only day she closed. But her reluctance wasn't just about that. "I planned on opening for half a day on Saturday, then giving Joe the afternoon to work."

"Won't Celeste be there? We won't be gone long. My mom would like to meet you. In fact, so would the rest of my family, but I don't care about them."

"Liar." They passed Mrs. Ramsey's but Kylie barely noticed the flowers. She was thinking about what he'd told her at dinner. "Wait. Is there something going on with your brothers? Did you guys have an argument or something?"

"Us? No. Why would you ask?"

"I don't know, I just remembered something you'd said about circumstances at home having changed."

Landon shook his head. "I'm the youngest brother, and crap rolls downhill. They're always yanking my chain about something. But no, we're tight."

"Okay," she said, "I just didn't want to be surprised. But seriously? Your mom wants to meet me? What did you tell her?"

"She's known about you for a while. I mean, it's no big deal. She wants to make sure I still have both legs, and I promised to come see them. You can meet the whole gang, kids, brothers, sister-in-law…everyone except my sister who lives in Utah."

The tummy butterflies had turned into hundreds of hummingbirds. He wanted her to meet his family? "I'm not sure I can. I mean, Celeste would have to make arrangements for her children. And she's still so new…"

"Maybe you could close all day Saturday and give Joe an extra few hours to work."

She just smiled.

"Hey, no pressure," he said, catching her hand and squeezing it. "Look, if you don't want to go then we won't."

She believed him, but could see that he was genuinely disappointed. "If I can't swing it, you could still go."

"Not without you."

They turned onto her driveway, her thoughts a complete jumble. She wanted to go, but she couldn't abandon her responsibilities. "I'll talk to Celeste. If she can work it out, I'd love to go."

"Excellent," he said with a heart-stopping smile and kissed the back of her hand.

Kylie melted like a stick of warm butter.

Chapter Fourteen

"You've got to be joking."

Rachel looked so shocked, Kylie thought there might be something bad in the fruit she'd brought for dessert, but she'd cut up everything fresh herself...

"Come. On." Rachel put the hefty bowl down on the dining room sideboard, and faced Kylie. "I was counting on you. It didn't even need to be chocolate. Turnovers. An apple fritter. A cupcake. You could have at least brought a cupcake."

Kylie met her friend's disappointed gaze. "I thought you said no sugar."

"No, *the doctor* suggested that. Because of the mood swings. Clearly he was wrong. I've had no sugar for a week. You tell me, do I seem like I'm in a good mood?"

"This is temporary," Kylie said, patting her arm. "Only a few more months, and you'll be able to have sugar again. You're strong enough to handle this."

"I'm not. I'm really not. You know what I dream about? Brownies. Your brownies." Rachel slumped, looking so defeated Kylie wanted to run to the bakery and grab a basket of goodies.

She didn't dare glance at Landon standing off to the side, even when he quietly cleared his throat. Kylie had thought fruit was the perfect answer for this small gathering, but then she looked at the sideboard. There were now three bowls of fruit lined up like soldiers. "Did you ask everyone to bring dessert?"

"I suppose I did," Rachel said with a shrug. "But when I asked you, I expected—"

"Things that would make you feel terrible?"

"Well, if you're going to put it like that..." Rachel sighed. "No. You're right. I can't have sugar. I'm already a hormonal, raging lunatic, so that makes everything swell. Sorry." She turned to Landon, who was juggling a bright bouquet of flowers and two bottles of wine. "Oh, those are beautiful." Finally, she smiled as she took the flowers.

"I'm glad you like them." Landon was either afraid to say anything more or was trying not to laugh. Kylie couldn't tell.

Rachel turned to go to the kitchen. "Let's just pretend that didn't happen. Okay?"

Kylie smiled. "Need help?"

"Always."

"Um, what should I do with the wine?"

Rachel's steps slowed. "That's something else I miss. Wine and margaritas."

Landon looked at Kylie, and they both laughed.

"Oh, shut up," Rachel said, sounding grumpy again. "Matt's huddling with the guys in the family room. Mind asking him?" She pointed to the open door across the foyer, even though the sound of male laughter gave it away.

"Thanks. If there's anything I can do to help, just holler." He gave Kylie a kiss on the lips, then walked away.

"Uh..." Rachel, who was also watching Landon's butt as he headed for the other room, finally glanced at Kylie. "Just a friendly kiss from a friend who's nothing but an old friend who's really friendly?"

"Now you can shut up. It *was* friendly, and now it's… friendlier. And don't get hysterical, but we're also going away for the weekend."

"When?" Rachel asked, her voice an octave higher than a minute ago.

"This weekend. I'm going to close the shop on Saturday afternoon and all day Monday. I decided I could use the break and Celeste volunteered to cover for me on Saturday morning."

"Well, hallelujah, I can quit worrying about you. The man's as hot as a firecracker and you were keeping him at arm's length?"

"Don't get too excited. We don't know where this is leading. If anywhere."

"Well, if you want my opinion, I think he's mad about you. And it's leading toward a very happy ending."

"Your opinion, Ms. Hormonal Nightmare? Now tell me who's here. Nikki and Trace?" Kylie started toward the kitchen, refusing to let this conversation continue. Thank goodness Rachel hadn't asked where they were going. Kylie wouldn't hide it from her, but she didn't want Rachel making a big deal out of it.

"Yes, and Mallory and Gunner. That's it. I don't know if Landon's met everyone, but I think they'll all get along."

"Of course they will," Kylie said.

The kitchen, like the rest of Matt and Rachel's house, was big and open, with beautiful cabinets, stainless steel appliances and an awesome island that would have dwarfed Kylie's kitchen all on its own. The color scheme was blue and gray, with hints of yellow that made it feel warm and cozy.

Mallory and Nikki both greeted her with hugs, and then the four of them got busy finishing up the sides. The brisket, which was the main course, was outside in the smoker—Matt's domain.

Baked potatoes with all the fixings, a tossed salad accompanied by Mallory's special dressing, corn on the cob and sangria for those who could imbibe were all in the mix. There was also a tray of biscuits waiting for the oven, and only then did Kylie realize that she should've thought to make a batch. It was Landon's fault. Just knowing the man was anywhere in the vicinity, much less in her bed, fogged up her thinking.

It didn't take long for Rachel to mention him, but Kylie was more prepared this time. "Look, he's only going to be here for a little while longer, so please don't embarrass him—and me—with insinuations, okay?"

"Don't look at us," Mallory said, exchanging a grin with Nikki, then tilted her head toward Rachel. "Tell that one."

Rachel made a face and slid the biscuits into the preheated oven. Then Nikki started talking about Rachel's plans for the nursery, and that's where the conversation stayed until the timer went off on the biscuits. By the time they finished putting all the food on the dining room table, Matt had already carved the brisket.

It all looked wonderful. She was seated across from Landon, between Gunner and Trace. Landon was between Mallory and Nikki, with Matt and Rachel at either end. Kylie wasn't sure how that had happened. She missed sitting next to him. He liked to touch her, whether it was to squeeze her hand or bump her thigh with his leg. But this way she got to look at him, so that wasn't a bad consolation prize at all.

"How's the counter coming along?" Trace asked.

"Slower than it should be," Kylie replied. "Joe is good

at what he does, but he works like he's got all the time in the world."

"Yeah." Nikki shook her head. "He did some repair work over at the Watering Hole, and it looks great, but Sadie watched him like a hawk. She even put time limits on his smoke breaks."

Everyone laughed. They all knew Sadie. She wasn't just the mayor, she owned the bar, and she didn't put up with guff from anyone. Hearing this about Joe didn't re-assure Kylie about leaving for the weekend.

"I know what he's like, and listen, if you need help at the shop, you know all you have to do is ask," Nikki said. "Better yet, tell him to get the lead out or you'll sic Sadie on him."

Kylie bit at her lip. "I might have to."

"By the way…" Nikki passed the corn and butter to an impatient Rachel, who was keeping up with the guys in the food department. "I ran into Celeste at the market. She loves working there."

"Not half as much as I like having her. She's taken a huge load off my shoulders. It's nice to be able to breathe again."

Mallory and Nikki both frowned at her. "Why didn't you say something?" Mallory said.

"You didn't think to mention that to your friends?" Nikki added. "We could've helped out in some way."

"Thanks, you guys," Kylie said, touched. She knew the offers were genuine. "Until recently I didn't realize how much time and energy I'd been pouring into the place."

Rachel stopped chewing long enough to grin. "Landon have anything to do with your epiphany?"

"Oh, just keep eating."

"That won't be a hardship for her," Matt said.

Rachel glared at him. "Lucky you're on the opposite end of the table, buddy."

"Okay, kids, behave yourselves. And no food fights." Trace gave them each a stern look. "I mean it."

Nikki reared back and looked at him. "You're the biggest baby here."

Everyone laughed at that, even Trace.

Landon caught Kylie's gaze and he winked. It was a simple gesture that meant nothing, but it filled her with so much joy and warmth it was almost silly. A month ago she would've been sitting here, odd person out. Though Rachel and the rest of the gang had always included her, and had never once made her feel out of place. But having someone of her own to share a joke with or exchange a look...this was new and different.

And heaven help her...she was going to miss him when he left.

Unprepared for the sudden wave of emotion sweeping over her, she bowed her head and pretended she'd dropped her napkin.

"Too bad Barry's going off to college," Landon said. "He's a hell of a good worker, and great with his hands. Joe would have some stiff competition."

"He's a nice kid," Matt said. "I'm glad he's doing a good job. How's your leg, anyway?"

"Doing a lot better. I hardly need the crutches at all anymore."

"That's right. You didn't bring them tonight." Rachel looked at Kylie. "Is he just being macho or is he okay without them?"

"Hey, wait a minute—"

Kylie was glad she could smile at something. "He's doing great."

Gunner, who'd been steadily eating, asked, "You think you'll make it to the finals?"

"So far I'm okay, but I've gotta hustle soon if I want to stay ranked. I'm thinking I'll get back in the saddle this weekend when we go see my family in Wyoming."

"What? Oh, no," Rachel said, swallowing quickly, her wide gaze shifting to Kylie. "That's where you're going?" Then she looked at Landon. "Don't tell me you're planning on dragging Kylie away from Blackfoot Falls. We just got to know her."

The quiet that settled didn't do a thing for Kylie's nerves, nor did the way Landon lowered his gaze so she couldn't see his eyes.

Matt cleared his throat. "If I recall you have a pretty big spread over there," he said. "Who's running things?"

Landon straightened, although she could see remnants of a slight flush on his face. "I've got two older brothers. Ranching is in their blood. They've been running things since my dad passed on."

"You planning on joining them when you leave the circuit?"

Landon put down his fork, his hesitation not surprising, but unsettling nonetheless.

"Yeah. Ranching is what I know. But I want to ride for a while yet. For as long as I can make some decent money, anyway. It must've taken a hell of a lot for you to get out when you were still on top. You miss it?"

Kylie wondered if Landon's deflection had been on purpose. It wasn't new information for her, but somehow she was receiving a different signal. The way he'd put it to Matt made it sound as if staying with the sport had more to do with ego than banking extra money. Or was she being touchy? She refilled her sangria and forced herself to relax.

"Yeah, right. I miss all the trips to the ER. The bruised ribs. The broken bones." Matt raised his eyebrows. "It served me well, though. I used the prize money to make some changes to the Lone Wolf. And it's allowed me the time to establish myself as a stock contractor."

"That's the thing about this sport," Landon said. "Whatever doesn't kill you, makes you wealthier."

Everyone laughed but Kylie.

"Gunner, you were in a similar situation," Matt said looking at the man. "I know you still take stunt jobs now and again. You miss the action, or is it strictly to keep union benefits?"

Gunner had to finish chewing. He hadn't said much since they'd sat down.

"Don't mind him," Mallory said dryly. "He hasn't eaten in months."

"Because you never cook." Gunner was fighting a grin, clearly expecting the looks of outrage from all the women.

The guys just shook their heads.

Mallory snorted. "Neither do you."

"Good point." Gunner chuckled, then looked at Matt and Landon. "I don't miss any of it, especially the traveling. Hard to pass up those benefits, though."

Well, Landon had done a fine job of throwing the focus off himself. Kylie took another sip of sangria. When she looked back at Landon, his gaze was on her, his expression one of concern.

"Hell, there are drawbacks to everything," Matt said. "Stock contracting isn't just sitting back and watching the dough roll in. A fair amount of travel is involved, which I don't like, and now, especially, with the baby coming…" He smiled at Rachel, reminding Kylie of Landon when he saw her after a long day. "But I'm training a couple of my men to follow the stock. I want someone out there while I concentrate more on bull breeding."

"Huh. I didn't know you were into that." Landon's interest had clearly been piqued.

"It's pretty fascinating stuff," Gunner said. "A lot goes into storing and shipping frozen—"

"Oh, please." Rachel slumped back in her chair. "Can we not talk about bull sperm now?"

Even Kylie had to laugh at that.

"Oh, we're definitely not," Mallory assured her, and then gave Gunner and Matt a pointed look. "You guys can discuss it all you want while you clear the table and clean up the kitchen. How's that?"

"Hey, wait a minute," Matt said. "I smoked the brisket."

"Yeah, and I taste tested it." Trace looked so serious it was hard to tell if he was joking.

Nikki put a hand to her heart. "Ah, my hero."

Talk of babies and a good deal of laughter dominated the rest of the meal. Kylie had no idea why tears were suddenly threatening. This was so much better than rodeo talk.

Except it would be far too easy to imagine what a baby might look like with Landon as the daddy, and oh, man she couldn't go there. Not now. Maybe not ever.

AFTER THE GUYS had cleared the table, Rachel chased them out of the kitchen. Kylie had already started loading the dishwasher which had helped her avoid Landon's questioning looks. No matter how hard she'd tried to hide her wobbly emotions, he clearly knew something was wrong. But she was already pulling herself together, and thankfully none of the other women had noticed.

Matt had turned on the big screen above the fireplace

to the Pendleton Round-Up—one of the three events Landon had been signed up for before breaking his leg. She only knew this because she'd heard Matt ask him about it.

Mallory and Nikki wrapped up the leftovers, and Rachel put the food away in the fridge. Her mood was much better now. She even joked about the mountain of fruit that was left.

Trace ducked his head in to ask Nikki if she wanted to see the new colt, and Mallory invited herself along as well. Rachel urged Kylie to go with them but she stayed and swept the floor.

Rachel dropped a wet dish towel into a basket and dried her hands. "Want to see what I've got for the nursery so far?"

Kylie was ashamed for hesitating even a second. "Of course."

"Unless you'd rather go watch rodeo with the guys," Rachel teased, and grinned at Kylie's wry expression. "That's what I thought. Come on."

Rachel led her through the foyer to the stairs. The den was to the right and while they could hear the low murmur of the TV, they couldn't see inside.

"Hey, while I've got you alone," Landon said. "I have a question I didn't want to ask in front of Rachel." His deep baritone didn't tend to carry, and he'd lowered his voice, but he had no way of knowing they were passing just outside the open door.

No doubt Rachel had heard him because she came to a dead stop. So did Kylie.

"Shoot," Matt replied.

"Do you have any regrets quitting when you did?"

Kylie sucked in a breath. So it hadn't been her imagination that he'd hesitated when asked about his future.

Did she want to hear Matt's answer, or worse, the follow-up discussion? She glanced at Rachel. It looked as if her eyes were a bit moist, and Kylie considered taking her arm and dragging her up the stairs with her.

"I need to go to the bathroom," Kylie whispered, and paused, silently pleading with Rachel to keep moving, but she only stepped aside for Kylie to pass.

Kylie hurried up the stairs, closed the bathroom door behind her, and just leaned against it for a minute. Maybe she should have listened. It was important to have the facts. Not that she was eliminating all possibility of a future with Landon, but she needed to be prepared so she could make sane decisions.

But it was just too soon for the dream to end.

"RACHEL? HONEY?"

"What?" she said, as Matt and Landon rushed out of the den.

She was standing on the first step. Crying. Like, really crying.

But since she didn't appear to be hurt, Landon wasn't sure if he should stay or make a hasty retreat.

"It's okay," Rachel said. "You can tell him the truth. That staying home all the time was never what you wanted. That you love going to the rodeos, and now you're stuck here with a crazy woman who never shuts up about chocolate."

The last few words were hard to understand through her sobs, but Landon had heard enough to know it was time for him to go. Though maybe he should've stuck around as a character witness. Matt hadn't said anything that Rachel should be upset about. Gunderson swore he wouldn't change a thing. The guy was obviously head-over-heels in love with his wife.

Landon went through the foyer and out the front door, although when he got outside he didn't see anyone. A couple of men were working near the barn and they motioned toward the stables.

He waved his thanks but he already knew Kylie hadn't gone with the others. Since she hadn't been with Rachel, maybe she was still in the kitchen. He sure hoped so and circled in that direction. Something was bothering her. It had started during dinner, and though she'd hidden it from everyone else, he'd seen through her forced smiles.

She wasn't in the kitchen, so he took another look around the Lone Wolf. It was an efficient, well-thought-out ranch. From the side of the house, he could see the barns, stables and corrals, and a good assortment of equipment sheds scattered about. Beyond the large cottonwoods he could see part of the arena Matt had built. The sucker was huge and had cost him a pretty penny, but Matt said he had no regrets, especially now that he was going into the business of producing and shipping frozen bull semen. And he'd been able to do it all because of his rodeo winnings.

Landon breathed in the cool mountain air. The area looked a lot like Wyoming. At least where he was from. They'd passed some nice pastureland on the ride over. He wondered if many ranches went up for sale.

This wasn't the first time he'd considered looking into what Blackfoot Falls had to offer. The thoughts had started a couple days ago when he'd been lying in bed with Kylie. She'd been sound asleep and the alarm was about to go off. And all he could think about was how much he was going to miss her when he left. He'd realized a part of him had hoped she wouldn't turn out to be the ideal woman he'd painted in his mind.

Damn, he sure hadn't been prepared for the opposite to be true. Made him regret some of the promises he'd made his family. Well, not promises, exactly, but they were all counting on him to return to Wyoming. But Kylie's life was here. That put him in a precarious position.

As he started his return trek around to the front, he heard voices in the kitchen. He walked closer to the window, and caught a glimpse of Kylie. She, Mallory and Nikki had surrounded Rachel, putting her dead center of a group hug.

It hit him again how entrenched Kylie had become in this community. Back in the day, she'd seemed like such a loner. But he'd realized, because of Gary, she just hadn't had many friends. Gary sure knew how to suck up other people's lives. Even Landon had often catered to the lazy bastard. Mostly though because he felt guilty about wanting Kylie.

Landon hadn't completely given up. He'd also thought that taking her to Wyoming would be a good chance to tell her that, while he thought joining the family ranch would no longer be the right move, he still wanted to live near them. To start a family there. But that was six hours away from her community, and it was hard enough to keep up with friends when they lived across town.

She loved it here. And she was loved, by a lot of people. Everyone wanted her to succeed. Including him.

Chapter Fifteen

Kylie stifled a yawn. They'd left early for Wyoming since Celeste had sworn up and down she could handle the brief Saturday morning rush by herself. Kylie had put up a sign alerting customers that the bakery would close at eleven and not reopen until Tuesday morning. A few of them had grumbled, but she'd expected that.

"Are we here?" she asked when Landon slowed the truck and turned off the highway onto a gravel road.

"Almost. The county owns this stretch of potholes that we always end up filling and grading ourselves. Another half a mile and we'll reach the driveway."

He wasn't exaggerating about the condition of the road. In fact, the deep ruts looked more like craters.

"Actually, this isn't too bad. You should see it in the spring after the snow melts. We have to rent a ferry just to go grocery shopping."

Kylie rolled her eyes. "You should've quit while you were ahead."

Grinning, he steered the truck around a particularly nasty pothole and then reached over the center console for her hand. "I hope I haven't built up the place so much you're disappointed when you see it."

"Are you kidding? This is gorgeous country. I doubt

it suddenly turns into a slum when we get to the Running Bear."

"Yeah, but this isn't really the best time of the year to see the ranch for the first time. It's been dry all summer and some of the grass is turning yellowish-brown and see those mountains?" He nodded to the east. "Those are the Bighorn Mountains. A month ago you would've seen nothing but emerald-green trees, and next month most of the leaves will be the most brilliant red and gold you've ever seen. And the wildflowers that pop out in spring? I promise you'll be drooling over 'em. I'd bet my truck on it. You just wait and see."

Kylie's breath caught. This wasn't the first time he'd talked about a future with her in it. And the way he spoke about the Running Bear, even the potholes, it was always *we,* as if there was no doubt he planned to return to the family ranch. How did any of that reconcile with his hesitation both with her and with Matt?

Coward that she was, she hadn't asked Landon about it. Even when he'd handed her the perfect opportunity on the ride home. No, she wouldn't call it cowardice. It was the walking on eggshells part of wanting each other. Her own missteps and his.

He'd noticed she'd gotten quiet and asked if anything was wrong. Kylie had blamed it on feeling bad for Rachel. While he'd accepted her answer, they'd driven most of the way back to her house in silence. Something was bothering him, too.

"By the way," she said, opting for a neutral topic even now, "why Running Bear Ranch? There must be a story behind it."

"Took you long enough." He made another turn. "This is the driveway. We'll be there in a minute. Anyway, in 1921 my great-great-grandfather, Jeb Kincaid, had purchased the land and built a house and barn. He'd grown up hearing stories of a young Arapaho man named Running Bear who, against all odds, had saved a whole village during a cavalry raid. But in the end, the native Americans lost the land to the US encroachment, so Running Bear barely got a mention, even though he saved a lot of innocent women and children. Jeb didn't think it was right that such a brave and selfless warrior's deed had gotten buried in history so he named the ranch in his honor. None of the Kincaids since then have seen any reason to change the name."

"Oh, that's a wonderful story. I like your great-great-grandpa. A lot. In fact you've all done the Kincaid name proud," Kylie said, smiling at his modest shrug and feeling a surge of emotion. Great. Just what she needed right before meeting everyone.

The long gravel driveway was in much better condition than the county road and it wasn't long before Kylie could see a couple of barns, three corrals, several sheds, and then there was the house, two stories high with large windows and a big porch.

Movement close to the nearest barn caught her eye and she watched as a man who looked a lot like Landon rolled out on a wheelchair.

"That's Chad. He's the handy one in the family. Give him a piece of wood and a hammer and there's nothing that guy can't do. Don't tell him I said that. His ego is big enough."

Kylie smiled at the affection in his tone. "So, you're on crutches, he's in a wheelchair—"

"I didn't bring the crutches, and no need pointing that out either."

"Of course not." She was well aware that Landon

didn't need them anymore. It was a giant reminder he'd be leaving her soon.

"I don't think I mentioned the wheelchair, did I?"

She shook her head, but didn't admit to her curiosity.

Landon parked the truck next to an older pickup loaded with fencing. "I'll tell you more about it later."

"Sure," she said. "He looks like you."

"Just make sure you tell him I'm the handsome one."

"Oh, your poor mom. Are your brothers still twelve, too?"

"Hey." His gaze moved past her and he nodded at the house. "Brace yourself."

A whole parade of people was coming out the front door. She spotted a woman who had to be his mother, and another dark-haired cowboy she took to be Martin, next to a tall redheaded woman wearing jeans, a long-sleeved T-shirt and a little one in a baby sling.

Bouncing around were also two kids who looked to be under ten. The girl had her mom's red hair.

Landon jumped out of the truck, and just as she was going to open her door, he did it for her. "What's this?"

"I aim to impress."

"Me?"

"No. My mom."

Laughing, Kylie let him help her down, and by then, the gang had arrived, and oh, boy…

"Long time no see, dude." Chad stopped his chair right next to Kylie. "No wonder he talks about you so much. His taste has vastly improved."

"You're not on crutches," his mother said, opening her arms.

Landon hugged her hard. "Told you I'd be okay."

"Well I missed you, and I noticed you still have a limp."

"It's almost gone."

She let him out of the hug, but briefly held on to his shoulders. "You look good. Your sister asked me to tell you that you owe her a call, and she's not going to put up with that nonsense."

"She should've called and told me herself. Would've saved me the trouble."

"I'll do you a favor and not repeat that," his mom said, giving Kylie an inclusive smile.

"Three weeks isn't that long. Anyway, let me introduce you ruffians. Kylie, this is my mother, Alison. That tall beauty is Chad's wife, Cindy, the bundle in her arms is Jenna and those two kangaroos are Liam and Fiona. The big guy is Martin, and don't believe anything he tells you. In fact, you shouldn't believe anything either of my brothers says about me."

"You didn't tell me there were rules," she said, "Mrs. Kincaid, it's wonderful to meet you. Landon's talked a lot about you. All of you, actually."

"Please, call me Alison," she said, taking Kylie's extended hand and wrapping it in both of hers. "And that's true about you, too."

Martin nodded and tried to hide the fact he was looking Kylie over. Cindy smiled, while managing to hold on to the baby and tug on Liam's collar to stop him from jumping. Chad leaned forward and grabbed hold of the boy's shirt, then pulled him to stand beside him.

Alison flicked a look at Martin. "I'm sure they have things in the back that you can help carry."

"But he's not even on crutches anymore."

"Don't start. Now, let's all go inside. They've been on the road for six hours."

"Seven," Landon said. "We stopped for lunch. But someone worked really late last night." He looked at

Kylie, his eyes full of warmth and a smile meant only for her. "I'll be right in. I've got to grab something from the backseat."

Kylie realized she had a rule or two of her own he needed to hear. Like not making her knees weak while they were visiting his family. She took a moment, then followed Alison and Cindy and a sleeping baby Jenna up the flagstone path to the porch.

Next to the steps was a sturdy-looking ramp. The whole layout was functional yet homey, a simple mix of dark wood and red brick, four rocking chairs with blue striped cushions, a double swing and tables for drinks.

Inside, the place surpassed her expectations. All of it had been built to a grand scale, sectioned off in groupings for more intimate conversations. The centerpiece was a huge stone fireplace.

There were accommodations made for easy wheelchair accessibility, all of which blended seamlessly, like the wider doors and the paths between furniture. The Kincaids' home wasn't as overtly Western as some of the ranch houses she'd been in. An antique hutch held gothic silver candleholders, and her peek at the dining room revealed an interesting mix of rustic and classic. In the living room, the family pictures drew her eye immediately, but she'd wait until things settled before she took a closer look.

They were in the kitchen when Landon caught up with them. He passed the basket of treats, still covered with a cloth, to Chad, and picked up Fiona. He gave her a loud kiss on her cheek.

Giggling, the little girl threw her arms around his neck. "I missed you, Uncle Landon. I got a rabbit. Do you want to meet her?"

"I do. But I want to make sure our guest is settled in first. What's her name?"

Fiona seemed confused. "Mom said her name was Kylie."

Landon grinned. "I meant the rabbit."

"Dora."

"Like the explorer?"

Fiona nodded vigorously. "She likes to hop a lot."

"I can't wait to get to know her. Now, I'm going to put you down so I can offer Kylie something to drink."

"I'd like hot chocolate," Fiona said.

"Me, too," her brother added, with a hop of his own.

Landon glanced at Cindy, who nodded.

"Anyone else for hot chocolate?"

Chad, Martin and Alison raised their hands. Kylie raised hers as well, then moved closer to Chad. "Thanks for holding that," she said. "May I?"

"If I get to taste what smells so good, sure."

"Of course you will." Turning to Alison, she said, "I brought you a sampling of pastries and things from my bakery. I'll let you decide when to pass them around."

"Oh, no, she's not the boss of me," Chad said and tried to snatch back the basket.

Kylie was too quick for him.

"Daddy thinks he's the boss of everybody," Fiona drawled with a pained sigh that made the adults laugh.

Landon snorted. "Yeah, we'll see about that."

"All right now, children. Behave," Alison said, then trained her blue eyes eagerly on the basket.

It was large. And very heavy, but once Kylie had gotten started making selections, she couldn't seem to stop. She'd included two of the German sweet loaves that Celeste had made, and then piled in a dozen vanilla and chocolate cupcakes, four kinds of cookies, cherry turnovers and assorted donut holes. There were two items missing and her heart sank. Then she remembered she'd put her signature chocolate dream cake and a chess pie in a paper bag. The pie was the only recipe she had from her grandmother. It was very old-fashioned, a variation of traditional custard made with cornmeal and a touch of vinegar. She'd get it later.

In the rush to check out the goodies, Martin shouldered past Landon, and the whole family swarmed Alison.

"Everything looks delicious. But there goes my diet," she said, sighing. "Tell you what, why don't you and Landon go upstairs and make yourselves comfortable while I start the hot cocoa. The guest rooms are all made up, so take your pick. And if you'd like to rest, please do. Dinner won't be ready for a couple of hours."

"Thank you." Kylie was a little surprised when Landon took her hand and tugged her to the door.

"There'd better be most of those treats left by the time we get back," he said.

"I wouldn't count on it." Martin reached in and snatched a donut hole. "Besides, you get this stuff all the time."

"True," he said and squeezed Kylie's hand. "Come on, we'll go the long way so you can see the family room."

It was spacious, with a huge big-screen TV and a wall display of trophies and ribbons of all sorts. Everything from 4H ribbons to Junior Rodeo trophies. There were three ribbons for sled hockey finals. "Chad?"

"Yeah. He's a maniac on ice."

She stopped to look at a photo. "Who's this with Martin? His wife?"

"She will be soon. Hailey's in Germany, where she's

a nurse at the Wiesbaden Army Health clinic. This will be her last tour, though."

"Is she from around here?"

"Nope. They met three years ago in Cheyenne while she was on leave. That's where she grew up. Most of her family still live there. Nice people."

"So…after they get married, will they live in Cheyenne, or here?"

Landon's brows went up. He couldn't have looked more surprised. "Here," he said, as if there was no other option worth considering.

And that confused her. Now that she knew Chad was in a wheelchair, it made it more difficult to understand why Landon wouldn't come home and help with the Running Bear. He'd said his brothers didn't need him, but how could he believe that? Something was off.

She put her confusion aside, for now. "Well, I don't blame them. It's a truly wonderful place," she said, turning to another photo of an older man proudly holding up his fresh catch. "Is this your dad?"

"Yep. He was so proud of that trout. It was the second largest ever caught in this county." Landon stared at the image for a moment. "We all miss him, but we're still tight. That doesn't always happen after a tragedy."

"Lucky. All of you. Very, very lucky." Kylie counted the number of trophies Landon had collected, perfectly illustrating his obsession with everything rodeo since his early teens.

"You don't talk much about your family."

"My family consists of my mother and my aunt Sally, both of whom you've met, and I think there's a great-uncle who lives in Idaho. I'm not sure if I ever met him. Mom has called him Lloyd and Floyd on different occasions. And my dad, I guess, but I barely remember him. He left when I was three."

"That's tough. I'm sorry."

"That's okay. I've got Rachel and the gang now." His slight wince made her wish she'd phrased it differently. "Can we go see our room. Although your mom said guest rooms?"

"She's leaving the arrangements to us. I vote we share."

"No argument from me."

Martin had left their bags on the landing, As they headed upstairs, Landon grabbed them both, then led her down a long hallway.

He stopped at a large window with a perfect view of the mountains. "That's Chad and Cindy's place."

Kylie moved closer to see the sprawling single-story house in the distance. "It looks huge."

"Well, yeah, three kids."

"Did they build it after the accident?"

Landon shook his head. "Two years before. But afterward we had it modified."

"Where does Martin live?"

"Here for now. When Hailey gets back, they're going to build their own place not too far from Chad's."

She couldn't shake her earlier confusion. "I have to ask," she said, lowering her voice. "With Chad using a wheelchair, I would've thought you'd be coming home for sure."

He nodded slowly, keeping his gaze on the horizon. "I know it's hard to understand, but it's complicated."

Kylie was starting to dislike that word. Did he still feel guilty for returning to the circuit?

"Bottom line is, they're doing fine without me." He shifted one of the bags. "Come on, let's go get settled."

They ended up in a spacious room with a queen bed, a small walk-in closet, and to her delight, a claw-foot tub that looked like heaven in the bathroom.

After they unpacked a few things, Kylie freshened up, eyeing the tub, letting her mind wander. It had been foolish, that flash of a thought that he might decide to move to Blackfoot Falls. She'd dismissed it quickly, and now that she saw his family, their ranch, it was an even greater flight of fancy. Even if Landon didn't return to the Running Bear, he'd want to stick close by.

A knock on the door reminded her that she hadn't given him his turn.

"Don't forget. You need to lie down, young lady."

"I will if you will."

After he'd finished in the bathroom, he stretched out next to her, pulling the folded quilt at the bottom over them both. She was exhausted, not just from working late, but anticipation and nerves about coming here. There was no reason at all to still feel edgy, as if she'd do something stupid. Or find out something—

She hadn't realized she'd closed her eyes until Landon scooted closer and wrapped her in his arms. "I'm glad you came with me," he murmured close to her ear.

"I am, too," she said, her lids drooping again.

Landon chuckled. "Sweet dreams, baby," he whispered, and that was the last thing she remembered.

THE DELICIOUS SCENTS of his mom's cooking drew them downstairs like a magnet.

A second before they entered the kitchen, Kylie said, "Is that—"

"Spaghetti and meatballs," he said as they joined the family. "My favorite meal."

"What?" Kylie asked. "Not steak and potatoes?"

"He's always been weird," Chad said, pulling out a chair for her.

"Um, I thought I'd help with—"

"Nope. Tonight, you're company. Tomorrow you can make us all breakfast."

Landon smiled, mostly because of Kylie's grin. She sat down, while the others put the finishing touches on the table. Garlic bread, salad and enough pasta to feed several armies.

She and Chad talked nonstop until everyone was seated. And then the conversation effortlessly shifted to include everyone. Already it felt as though Kylie belonged.

He hadn't had a lot of women over. Two, altogether. Shelly had been his girlfriend in college. She'd been great, but her sense of humor was a little stiff and she was more interested in garden parties than the rodeo. She'd ended up with a pediatrician in Los Angeles.

Now, here was Kylie. Who laughed so hard at one of Martin's jokes, she almost choked on a meatball, which caused quite a scene. Oh, yeah. She fit in his family like a missing puzzle piece.

If only things were that simple.

"We've heard a lot about your new coffee bar," Alison said, passing the garlic bread. "Very enterprising. I'm assuming it doesn't have a lot of competition out there?"

"Nope. I'll be the only espresso service for miles around. And you'd be surprised how many cowboys have asked me if they can get hazelnut lattes."

Chad cleared his throat and looked at his plate, while his wife cracked up. But he rallied. "I keep hearing about these bench seats and tables."

"Oh, come on…" Landon wanted to clock him.

"Just a word of advice. Make him sit on everything first. That way, *he'll* be the one to fall on his ass."

"Boys." Alison had a glare for each of her sons. "Language."

Chad glanced at his kids and nodded. "He's my brother and I love him, but he doesn't know a hammer from a wing nut."

"What?" Kylie said, putting down her fork. "No, quit it. He's doing a great job."

"You've tried them out?" Martin asked.

"Hush, you two." Alison stood up and took Landon's plate, serving him a healthy second helping.

"Well, no. It's going to be a surprise."

"I'll say," Chad muttered.

Landon shook his head. "One thing. I asked you clowns for one lousy thing, and you just had to shoot off your big mouths."

"Hey, the lady deserves to know the good and the bad," Martin said. "It's only fair."

Kylie frowned, looking worried. "You guys are joking, right?"

"Yes," Landon cut in.

"Nope," Chad said at the same time. Then he said, "Ouch" when Cindy gave him a hell of a pinch.

"Yes," Martin said, loudly. "We're joking. I'm sure he and whoever he has helping him are doing a fine job."

"Besides," Liam said, a fair amount of pasta sauce smeared on his chin. "No one rides broncs like Uncle Landon. He's the best in the whole world."

Landon grinned.

Until he caught a glimpse of his mother's troubled expression.

Chapter Sixteen

After dinner, Landon got the cake and pie from the truck, then he and Kylie joined the family at cards while everyone got sugar highs. For Kylie, the best part was holding Jenna while Cindy put the older two kids in Grandma's bed. The baby was awake, staring at her with curious blue eyes that seemed to understand just how much Kylie wanted a little one just like her.

Right after Jenna had fallen asleep, Chad approached. "There's a crib in Mom's bedroom," he said. "She won't sleep for too long, and then we'll take her home."

"She's the sweetest thing."

He smiled with a father's pride. "She's a beauty. Thank goodness she takes after her mother."

Kylie put her carefully into Chad's arms, and was impressed with how he handled her so well while maneuvering the wheelchair. It didn't take him long to return, and take his place in the card game.

Kylie joined in again, too, but she was far more interested in Landon's hand on her thigh, and the looks he sent her way. He seemed so at peace, so content.

She completely understood.

After such a long day, the two of them called it quits just after ten, when Jenna announced her presence over the baby monitor.

If it weren't for the fact that tomorrow was a regular work day for Chad and Martin, Kylie probably would've fought off her yawns and stayed up all night. She liked his family so much. And the brothers... Oh, how she used to yearn for siblings so they could tease each other, support each other and not feel so alone.

The real revelation had been watching Landon with the kids. He'd been rough and tumble with Liam, who worshipped his uncle and was already practicing to throw a lariat over a miniature set of bull horns in the backyard. But Landon had almost made her cry when they'd met Dora, the black-and-white bunny who was almost as big as Fiona. Landon had listened as if the bunny's life story was the most interesting thing he'd ever heard, and together, he and Fiona had fed Dora lettuce and then, in a surprise twist, the rabbit had pooped right on Uncle Landon's lap. He didn't even get upset.

It was envy, pure and simple, that ran through Kylie as she waited for him to join her in bed. Until she remembered the look on Alison's face when they'd started talking rodeo.

Landon, wearing absolutely nothing, walked slowly toward her, then climbed into bed, and it not only distracted her, but it created quite a dilemma. They were both exhausted, and they were getting up very, very early the next morning. When he couldn't hold back a jaw-cracking yawn, she knew the answer.

"Tell me more about Chad's accident," she said, as she ran her hand down his hard chest just below where her head rested, memorizing the muscles and purposefully skipping more sensitive areas.

Landon shrugged. "He didn't fall all that far, but hard enough to damage his spinal cord. Even though Martin didn't find him right away, the doctors said it wouldn't have mattered, the damage was already done."

"He seems so…well adjusted. Cindy, too."

"Oh, she was devastated. Fiona was really little, and Liam wasn't much bigger. Chad was inconsolable. He blamed himself for being reckless, crap like that. But mostly, he wasn't sure he could call himself a real man anymore."

"Well, obviously he can still have children, so there's that…" She sighed. "I hope that wasn't too—"

"Nope. You're right. He was lucky in that sense. I came home the next day, and none of us let up on encouraging him to fight, even when he was at his worst. But it was his kids that really made the difference. Thinking about how they'd be embarrassed about their dad if he didn't make the most of his life. Then he hit rehab like a man on a mission. Nothing could stop him. Those muscles he's got now, that upper body strength? That's because he still never lets up.

"We found out how we could make the ranch easier for him, adapted the tractor, the baler, mostly the big equipment. At the same time, we modified his house, and put in ramps here at Mom's. Luckily, his house was single story. Later, he got involved with other farmers and ranchers who were paraplegic, and then he discovered the hockey team. It does him a world of good, although it's terrifying to watch. Especially for my mom."

Kylie bit her lip. Had Landon not seen his mother's face at dinner? Alison clearly wasn't all that keen on him riding rodeo either. "I can't imagine what a difficult transition that was. And what kind of bravery it takes to not let it drown you."

Landon yawned again, which made her yawn. "Know what the biggest help was, aside from family? He rides.

He's got a mean old stallion named Blade, and Chad saddles him up every morning. He told me it's the one thing that lets him feel like he's moving again. Like he's walking and running. He even joins the men for the yearly roundup."

"Wow. That's inspiring."

"Humbling," Landon murmured.

"That, too." She could see that his brothers were doing fine, but surely Landon coming home could help make life easier for everyone. "He's really grabbed life by the tail, hasn't he?"

Landon rolled onto his side, brushed her cheek with the back of his hand. "I'm proud of him. Proud to be a Kincaid."

"I don't wonder," she said, and then his kisses changed the subject.

AFTER BREAKFAST THE next morning, the men saddled up to go move the two-year-old heifers to a fresh field and round up strays. Cindy suggested Kylie take an ATV and go with them, and she'd ride up to meet her later.

Landon rode Flash, staying close to Kylie as his brothers led the way to the back pasture, where two hired hands were already at work replacing cedar posts along the fence line. Chad rode ahead, so anxious to jump into the action that he'd already cornered a stray calf.

Kylie could see how good Landon felt being back in the saddle. She shooed him off when he seemed reluctant to leave her on her own.

When Cindy arrived, Kylie hopped off her ATV, and they perched on the hood of the pickup the hired hands had used to haul the wire fencing. For a while all Kylie did was stare at Landon. He rode as if he was born to do it, and the joy on his face, no matter what they were doing, was obvious even from a distance.

She noticed that Cindy was watching her husband, a little smile turning up her lips.

"Landon told me about what happened to Chad, but I didn't get it until now," Kylie said. "The strength and agility he has takes my breath away. I don't know what he was like before, but he's one heck of an athlete now."

"Ironic that his main job before all of this was accounting."

Kylie laughed.

"I'm not kidding. That's what he studied in college. He takes care of the finances for all of us."

"My admiration just grew. That's the part of being a business owner that sucks the most."

"I hear that," Cindy said, right before her husband was nearly dragged off his saddle by a furious cow.

Kylie's gasp caught in her throat.

Cindy shrugged. "Yeah. Sometimes it's scary, and I can't help but worry. But I've never asked him to stop doing what he loves. I was there when he felt useless, and that was worse than anything. Well, you know what I mean. These Kincaid boys are proud. I swear Chad gets in the worst scrapes playing hockey, but I just cheer my fool head off. I mean, look at that crazy dope, grinning like he got the brass ring."

"Yeah," Kylie said, her thoughts racing. She did know that Landon wasn't one to sit idly by. "Can I ask you something? Just between us, and if you don't feel comfortable with the question, then please just—"

"Go ahead, ask away." Cindy wore sunglasses, something Kylie should've considered. She hated to think what her eyes might be giving away.

"Does Alison approve of Landon riding rodeo? Wait. Approve is the wrong word."

Cindy nodded. "I know what you mean. I'd say it's more like she grins and bears it. Like when she watches Chad play hockey. It's hard to do, but she wouldn't hold either of them back."

Kylie didn't know how to respond so she just watched Landon race off into the foothills. "Where's he going?"

"Most likely he's after a calf. How do you feel about the rodeo?"

"I hate it."

Cindy smiled. "Even before he broke his leg? Because I think that upset Alison more than she lets on. Understandable, though, after what happened to Chad."

"It does bother me that he could get seriously hurt. I try not to think about it too much. Although, that's not exactly what I was wondering about. It's just that it's hard to tell what he's thinking, about the future, I mean. He'd always seemed so sure of what he wanted—you know, to return to ranching. But lately, I don't know if he'll ever give up the rodeo. I mean, of course he'll have to stop at some point. But it's odd that he's wavering. In the past, if he had a plan he stuck to it."

Frowning, Cindy studied her for a moment, then gazed off toward the foothills where he'd disappeared.

"Maybe I'm wrong."

"You're not," Cindy said. "Even when he was young Landon could be very focused. As far as ranching, he's always been happiest sitting in a saddle. And I don't mean trying not to get bucked off. Have you asked him about it?"

"He said he wanted to ride as long as he could. That he needed to sock away more money."

"Well, dammit," Cindy said on a sharp exhale. "I

shouldn't be surprised. Since Chad's accident he's sunk a small fortune into the Running Bear—"

Landon emerged from the trees on the heels of a surly calf, and they both turned to watch him. Minutes ticked by, and great as it was to be able to see him in his element, Kylie knew the opportunity for Cindy to say more had passed. Or maybe she'd decided the information was too personal to be sharing.

Kylie could fill in some of the blanks, though, and it was quite a relief. If Landon had been helping out his family financially, which didn't surprise her, then he likely did need to replenish his savings.

She knew there were still things they needed to talk over, lots of things. Yet, this was their time with his family, something she'd never dared to dream about sharing.

There'd be time to discuss everything later, after they got back to Blackfoot Falls. If she could unwrap herself from the cocoon she'd built around having Landon in her life.

LUNCH HAD CONSISTED of sandwiches and fruit, so by the time the sun started to dip behind the mountains, everyone was starving. And even though Landon had taken quite a few breaks to stretch his legs, he knew he'd reached his limit in the saddle. Kylie had returned to the house earlier and spent the last hour helping his mom in the kitchen. Dinner was another great meal, but he was beginning to worry about his budding addiction to her biscuits.

When he got up to refill the water pitcher, his mother joined him at the sink. "She's wonderful," she whispered. "And I can see she's crazy about you."

He winced. It wasn't that things weren't great between

them. It was the future that had him worried. "I'm glad she could get away from the bakery for a few days, but—"

"You think I don't see how you feel about her?"

"Mom. Stop. It's complicated."

She gave him a quick hug. "Isn't everything?"

Once he was back at the table, ready to dig into a big slice of Kylie's chocolate dream cake, Martin, who was sitting next to him, bumped his shoulder and nearly sent the forkful of cake onto the wood floor.

"Sorry about that. Listen, I've got a question for you. In fact we all do. How serious were you about buying some land in the area?"

Landon put down his fork, tempted to look for Kylie's reaction. "Why ask me now? Can't we just enjoy dinner?"

Martin reared his head back. "I didn't know it was a touchy subject. Guess that means you're still going to be stubborn about it."

"I'm not discussing this now. Jesus, you act like I've got one foot in the grave already. I broke a few lousy bones, doesn't mean my career is over."

"Whoa, dude. This has nothing to do with the rodeo. Don't get your panties in a twist."

Cindy stood. "Come on, kids. Let's go wash your face and hands."

Landon sent her a look of apology. "Hey, listen to your mom," he told Fiona when the girl ignored her. "Later, we'll go tell Dora a bedtime story."

Fiona giggled. "You're funny, Uncle Landon."

"Yeah, a real barrel of laughs," Chad muttered.

"Oh, for goodness sakes, what's gotten into you boys?"

"Jeez, Mom, I was only teasing," Chad said. "We're all good. Right, baby brother?"

Landon couldn't help but laugh. "Sure, you pain in the ass."

Their mom sighed. "Kylie, I promise you I raised them to have manners."

"Actually, I find this pretty entertaining," Kylie said, but her voice sounded off.

"That's because you don't have brothers." Landon sneaked a look at her. She gave him a tight smile.

"Okay. Seriously," Martin said. "The reason I brought this up is because you'd mentioned something about buying land in the area. Well, Gutierrez is going to be selling off a thousand acres, and it just so happens it's the parcel on the east side adjacent to us. You should go talk to him before he puts it on the market. I bet he'd offer you a good deal."

Landon was pissed at himself for losing his cool. But this was tricky. He had too many things to work out yet. "Yeah, okay. Thanks. I'll swing by the next time I'm here."

Chad glanced at Martin before he turned to Landon. "Hey, we know you won't need it for a while, but at least find out how much they're asking." When Landon just nodded, Chad added, "Hell, you know my opinion. I think you should stick with rodeoing for as long as you can. Especially after the year you've just had. But come on, how lucky is it that some land right next door is available? Unless there's more to you not wanting to come back to the Running Bear. You still wanna go your own way, we won't stop you."

He gave his brothers a look that practically screamed *shut up* but all that did was make Kylie squirm, and his brothers look like a couple of idiots. If he'd just taken a moment to shift in his chair, Kylie wouldn't have seen a thing, dammit.

It's not that he wasn't interested in the land. Chad was right. All in all it was perfect. But in Landon's dream,

Kylie was with him, and now, he wasn't sure what to do about that. The bakery, her friends, the life she'd built after being so beaten down she might never have gotten up again. Was it even fair for him to ask?

He sure as hell didn't want to have this discussion right now. "Mom, what did you decide about buying that piano we looked at? I'd sure love to hear you play again."

Her face brightened. "I'm so glad you mentioned it. I wanted to show you something. Would you all mind if I stole him for a few minutes?" She'd already pushed back in her chair. "We won't be long, then you can finish your cake."

Generally, Landon could read her, but not now. Still, he was pretty sure this had nothing to do with a piano. He was too old to be pulled aside and lectured. Although that didn't always stop her. He followed her into his dad's old office.

The second his mom told him to shut the door, Landon knew he was in trouble.

Chapter Seventeen

His mother turned to face him. "You have to stop sending checks," she said, and held up a silencing finger when Landon tried to object. "It has nothing to do with you being laid up. I told you months ago that we're doing great." She went around the desk and opened a drawer. "Chad has everything he needs. We all do. Frankly, I don't think my heart could take it if he found one more *toy* to rig up so that he can risk his neck. Plus we're flush. Receivables are up. The ranch is doing very well."

He took a moment to really look at her as she searched inside the drawer. Her blond hair was shorter than the last time he'd seen her, and she'd put on some of the weight she'd lost after his dad's death. She looked ten years younger than she had just a few years ago.

"I'm glad you brought it up. I heard the same thing from Chad, and I'm really pleased," he said, "but that doesn't mean you can't squirrel some money away for an emergency."

"For goodness sakes, don't you know your own mother? Do you think for one minute I haven't set aside a comfortable nest egg?"

It was time for him to just accept they no longer needed his help. Which was a good thing. He skimmed a hand over the worn brown leather of his dad's old chair. "So, you're still using this, huh?"

"Of course I am." It appeared she found what she was looking for and closed the drawer. "When was the last time you were in here?"

"It's been a few years." The shelves were still crammed with books covering every topic from animal husbandry to global weather patterns. Even his dad's old Rolodex still sat on the corner of the polished mahogany desk. And the ancient lava lamp never failed to make Landon smile.

"I thought about replacing the rug. Parts of it are so worn you can't even tell it's a map." She shrugged. "I just can't bring myself to get rid of it."

"Well, for what it's worth, you know Dad would want you to do whatever makes you happy."

She smiled. "The same goes for you. That's all we ever wanted for you."

He looked up. "I know that, Mom," he said, searching her eyes as she came around the desk to stand beside him. "Is there a reason you think I'm not happy?"

Tilting her head slightly, she frowned at him. "I have two questions for you, and I'd like honest answers. Regardless of whether you think it's any of my business or not."

Landon grinned. "There's the mother I know and love."

"I'm being serious, honey."

"Okay." He figured he knew one of the questions. "Ask away."

"I was always under the impression that you'd be quitting the rodeo and settling down by now. You've been winning, so I understand why you might be pumped up, but you were always such a sensible boy. This talk about riding to the bitter end doesn't sound like you. Especially after finding someone as great as Kylie." She paused, but he could tell she wasn't finished with him.

"On top of that," she said, "first you were all gung ho about coming back to help your brothers. Then six months ago you started talking about wanting your own ranch. Frankly, we were all shocked, and yes, disappointed, but you assured us you planned on living nearby."

Yeah, it had been the perfect solution. Until Kylie.

Landon stretched his neck to the side. This conversation was getting way more intense than he'd expected. And hell, she hadn't even asked him anything yet.

"Chad thought—we all thought you'd be thrilled that Carlos wants to sell. It couldn't be more ideal. So, I have to wonder if this change in attitude is because you don't have enough money."

"No, Mom. I'm fine."

Undeterred, she narrowed her eyes. "You've been far too generous with us. If Chad ever found out *all* the funds came from you and not from an insurance policy—"

"He won't know if you don't tell him."

She didn't care for his tone and let him know with a stern look. In all honesty, he hadn't meant to sound abrupt.

"So, have I misjudged Kylie? Is she encouraging you to go after that million-dollar prize?"

Landon snorted a laugh. "That's the last thing she wants," he said. "I know she'd be a lot happier if I never competed again."

"Well, maybe you should think about that."

Sighing, he put an arm around her. "Look, I know this is hard for you. After what happened to Chad, then I break a leg and now you're touchy and thinking the worst. I have a good shot at going to the finals, and maybe taking the title. Yeah, I want it, and the gold buckle and definitely the million bucks. But I won't be stupid, okay? I promise you."

She gave him a grudging smile. "See? That wasn't so hard, was it? Here…" She slipped something in his breast pocket. "Before I forget. Now, the other question—"

"I'm pretty sure you worked in both questions already." He lowered his arm and looked her in the eye. "Don't try sandbagging me now."

"I'm doing no such thing," she said with an exasperated huff. "That was merely a compound question."

Landon laughed. "Nice try. Now, what is this in my pocket?" He fished around and pulled out torn pieces of paper. Not just paper, pieces of a check. His check. The last one he'd sent her?

The door opened, startling them.

"I've been looking all over for you," Fiona said with a big sigh. "Hurry up so we can watch movies."

"What did I tell you about knocking first?"

Fiona gave her grandmother a gap-toothed grin.

"Movies," Landon muttered. "What kind of movies?" As if he didn't know.

"One second, honey, we'll be right there."

Fiona left with a frown that said they'd better hurry.

"Mom—"

"Let me ask this, please. Why aren't you coming back home? Does it have to do with the rodeo? Or with Kylie?"

Landon wasn't ready to talk about his confusion over Kylie, and what to do about that. All he knew for sure was that he loved her, and wanted to be with her. Somehow. And make her happy in the process.

"Look, you just said things are going really well here. And I can see that's true. Even though I'd already made the decision, watching Chad this morning convinced me I'm right. He's such a vital part of the operation. He feels needed and he is. If I were to come back, we'd risk shifting the dynamics. Chad could end up feeling useless and slip back into that terrible depression again. I won't take that chance."

His mother bowed her head, eyes closed. She took a deep breath, then looked at him again. "I'm not sure I agree, but I admire the thinking that went into your decision. Maybe, and it's just a suggestion, you could talk to your brother?"

"I've got a lot to think about, Mom." Understatement of the year. All those promises he'd made to his family about returning. And then Kylie happened. So happy and rooted in her new town. He gave his mom a one-armed hug as he walked her to the door. "We'll work it out. Okay?"

Man, talk about being between a rock and a hard place.

KYLIE PUT ON her best face as she helped Landon and Martin clear the table, while Alison put away the food. Thankful that Chad and Cindy were tending to the kids, she even managed to ask Alison about her musical background. But inside, Kylie was tense. Landon's brothers were making it very difficult to put off the honest conversation she needed to have with him. Maybe this was the universe's way of ripping the cocoon from her whether she liked it or not. But she still didn't want to have the discussion here.

"I'll get the dishes," she said, touching Alison's arm when she stationed herself at the sink.

"You don't have to do that." Alison patted her hand. "You're supposed to be out of the kitchen this weekend, and you've already done so much."

"I can't help it. Kitchens call to me. And believe it or not, I find washing dishes relaxing."

Landon laughed. "You could've mentioned that all those times you made me clean up."

"What would've been the fun in that?"

Martin chuckled.

Landon gave her a look that prompted her to step back. "You see, Mom?" he said to Alison, while keeping Kylie in his crosshairs. "You thought she was such a nice girl."

His mouth was curved in that sly half grin that never failed to make Kylie shiver. She swallowed hard.

Martin made a hasty exit.

Alison smiled and slipped the dish towel off her shoulder. "Make sure he helps you."

"Oh, he will," she said, a second before Liam yelled for "Uncle Landon."

"Ah, gee, sorry sweetheart. I'd love to help but duty calls." He put his hands on her waist and dipped his head for a kiss. Not just a quick peck, either.

Kylie kissed him back, then remembered his mom was there. By the time she'd pulled away, Alison was gone.

It didn't matter. Kylie still shooed him away. "Go. Get out. I need some Zen."

"Some what?" Landon leaned back, laughing.

"Zen."

"Since when…"

"Since right now."

Liam yelled for his uncle again, and she practically pushed Landon out of the kitchen with both hands pressed against that broad chest she'd come to know quite intimately. And which she absolutely couldn't think about right now.

She wasn't the type who could meditate, but then she'd never really tried it. Three minutes later she understood why. Her mind was buzzing even more than it had before. Trying to clear her head was a fool's errand anyway.

The trouble with having a light shining on her fantasies was that the light wasn't very discriminating. It showed everything.

Like the fact that she'd fallen in love with Landon. Maybe fallen wasn't even the right word.

Her feelings for him hadn't just started when he'd come to stay at her house. Lord, he was so much the man she'd wanted when she thought of forever, it squeezed her heart. Whatever it was that he was holding back, he clearly didn't want to share it with her. Yet. At least he hadn't made empty promises. That was something… But the clock was ticking.

Which meant that she had to get her head out of the clouds, and figure out exactly what she wanted. Could she make peace with Landon being on the road so much? Traveling to rodeos had never been something she'd considered, but it wasn't out of the question if it meant seeing him.

But what about the bakery? She couldn't just take off whenever she wanted. And she wasn't making enough money to justify hiring someone else.

And what about later? If things really got serious between them? No. No good would come of getting ahead of herself.

She'd just wanted the illusion to last. Possibly for the rest of her life.

KYLIE TRIED to compartmentalize her feelings for the rest of the evening. But Landon didn't make it easy. Even after the slight awkwardness at dinner there'd been so much laughter, such closeness.

It got surreal, though, when Alison brought out old movies. Family movies. Not just of her grandchildren but of her sons and daughter, despite the guys' loud objections.

Watching Landon as a little tyke, so rambunctious he must have been a terror, brought a smile to Kylie's face. As for his affinity for horses, she counted only two shots of him without a horse somewhere in the picture.

But right in the middle of watching his parents' twentieth anniversary party, the smell of the room changed. Jenna, the adorable little muffin, could have knocked down a barn with the stink.

"Sorry," Cindy said, moving forward to rise from the couch.

"I've got it," Landon said, snatching the baby from her.

Kylie expected anything but Cindy's casual "Thanks," as she settled back down. Landon walked with Jenna at arms' length, grumbling at her for being a little stinkpot, but smiling the whole way.

Kylie looked at Cindy, who grinned. "Yep. He got used to that with Liam and Fiona. He does a way better job than Martin."

"Hey," Martin said, although it was a bit mumbled as he was polishing off the goody basket.

"Which," Cindy continued, "is almost certainly on purpose. Landon never blinked. Just jumped into the deep end of the pool, and that was that. He's really something, that one. I have to be honest and tell you I got the best one, but he comes close."

"Hey!" Martin said again, scowling.

"You've got a window to learn all about what you'll need when Hailey gets back," Cindy said, arching a brow at him. "Don't blow it."

The movie went on, the music Country and Western, the dancing an uncoordinated mess with everyone from toddlers to grandparents, and they all looked so happy.

Even after Landon returned and sat next to her with their thighs touching, Kylie remained quiet, not trusting that her voice wouldn't quiver. Soon enough, they would both have to lay down all their cards.

The only problem was, she might end up with the losing hand.

Chapter Eighteen

They arrived in Blackfoot Falls midafternoon on Monday, and Kylie couldn't wait to see the new counter so they went straight to the bakery. A tarp hung in the window, which made sense. Not only did people tend to ignore the Closed sign, too many busybodies would be peering inside and bothering Joe. He was just getting ready to lock the door when they pulled to the curb.

He waited for them, then passed the key to Kylie. "Guess I won't be needing this anymore."

"You're finished?"

"Said I would be, didn't I? Have a look."

Kylie's excitement woke her up completely, after having slept for most of the return trip home.

"Wow, Joe. You did an amazing job." Kylie drew her hand over the sleek gray and black surface, trimmed with polished ash. It wasn't granite but it looked and felt like it. She glanced over her shoulder at Landon. "Isn't it beautiful?"

"Gotta admit, it came out better than I pictured," he said, bending over to get eye-level with the lower ledge where customers would be able to set down their drinks. "You can't even tell this isn't part of the original counter."

Joe looked pleased, but then shook his head. "It's a wonder I got anything done at all. Didn't get a moment's peace, what with Rachel McAllister and Celeste yammering at me."

"Rachel was here?"

Joe eyed Kylie. "I figured you sent them."

"Celeste was supposed to work half a day on Saturday, but other than that, no."

"Well, glad you like it. Now I gotta get to my other job."

"You have any material left?" Landon asked. "In case we want to use it for trim?"

"I have scraps in my truck. Trim would be just about the only use for them. I cut the measurements close to keep the cost down. By the way…" He stopped at the door and reached into the pocket of his coveralls. "Might as well give you the final bill."

Landon reached for it the same time she did.

Kylie snatched it first and almost choked at the amount. It couldn't possibly be right. She distinctly remembered telling Joe to let her know if the material or labor exceeded his quote by more than ten percent before he proceeded.

He already had his hand on the doorknob. "If you can pay the balance by the end of the week I'd be much obliged."

Just as she was about to call him back, Landon gave her hand a squeeze. "No problem," he said to the man. "We'll get it to you tomorrow."

Joe had barely closed the door behind him, when Kylie lit into Landon. "What is wrong with you? Not only is this more than we agreed upon," she said, waving the paper at him, "you had no business interfering."

Landon looked surprised at first, then he smiled. "Look, you're still tired from the weekend," he said, as he cupped her cheek with his big hand. "I understand my family can be overwhelming at times—"

"None of that has anything to do with it." She inched back and his hand fell away. "I know you're trying to help but—"

"It's my fault. I asked Joe to order something for me and I think he added it to your bill by mistake. So I figured I'd look it over before saying anything to you."

"Added what? Material for the tables and bench seats?"

"No, something for me, personally. For my truck. I need sheltered cargo space."

She wasn't sure she believed him, but why would he lie?

"May I?" He nodded at the bill.

Reluctantly, Kylie handed him the invoice, the ringing of the bell above the door reminding her that she hadn't locked it.

Patty stuck her head in. "I just clocked out and didn't know if you were open…"

Kylie sighed, still thinking about the bill. "Come on in, but I don't know if I can help you."

"I was hoping you still had turnovers. Oh. Guess not. Nice counter, though."

"Sorry, we just got back. Celeste only made enough Danish and muffins for the motel this morning."

Patty looked over at Landon. "We wondered where you were. You haven't been to your room in a while."

Kylie stared at him. He seemed startled but didn't correct Patty.

"Well, you two look beat," Patty said. "See you tomorrow."

Kylie summoned a smile, then watched as Landon locked the door behind Patty.

She got tired of waiting for him to say something. "I thought you checked out."

"I was going to, but I saw Kevin in the lobby that morning. That's when I realized if I gave up the room and people saw me around town, they'd know I was staying with you."

"So?"

"I did it so there wouldn't be gossip—"

"I didn't ask you to." While he claimed he needed to save money, he'd been needlessly paying for a motel room.

Her gaze caught on a sticky note on the back shelf and she suddenly remembered she had to prep for tomorrow. She could have cried. There was no way she'd get through it still being this exhausted.

Landon was staring at her with what appeared to be concern. But did she really know what that looked like on him? He didn't have to lie about the motel room. Unless keeping it while he stayed with her made it feel less like a commitment. Though she'd never given him the impression she expected anything from him.

Dammit, going to meet his family had been a mistake. A giant, hurtful mistake.

Just as he took a step toward her, she pulled out her cell phone and started texting, her focus never leaving her flying fingers. First, to Celeste, letting her know she was back and that everything looked wonderful.

"Kylie…"

Next, she started typing a thank-you to Rachel, but her phone rang… Rachel's ring tone, so Kylie answered. "So, I hear you were nagging Joe to finish up," she said. "And that we're down a dozen brownies."

"Hey, I didn't touch anything. I sniffed. Cried buckets. Moped a lot, but I didn't take one bite. Anyway, doesn't the counter look great? By the way, I know you know how to use the espresso machine, and I'm allowed to have lattes as long as I don't add sugar, so anytime…"

Kylie chuckled. "I just got back. I haven't even been home yet."

"I want details. Everything from the drive to the family to the long Wyoming nights."

"Yeah, well, sometimes we just can't get what we want. But I'll make sure you're the first to know when the coffee bar is operational."

Rachel quieted for a moment. "You all right, kiddo?"

"I'm fine. Just tired. I'll be in touch, okay?" Kylie hung up, anxious to leave, ready to take a long, hot bath and stop her thoughts from beating up on her.

"Should we head home?" Landon asked, wisely keeping some distance between them.

"Yeah. Everything looks good here."

"I admit Joe did a great job. I can't wait to see the whole thing finished. The bench seats and tables. You're going to have customers lining up all day."

She forced a smile. "I'm sorry for snapping at you," she said, even though she wasn't. But she probably wasn't being fair to him either. Just…she needed a little more time to process things. "I wasn't kidding when I said I was tired."

"I know, sweetheart." He put an arm around her shoulders. "Let's get you into bed."

She shivered. Despite her anger, her confusion, her certainty that things were about to implode, his touch still managed to turn her into a lovesick teen. It would have been easy to walk ahead to the door, but there was comfort in his scent, his body so close to hers.

Before they made it out, someone tried the knob, then

knocked. Kylie held back a moan. At least it was just Sadie.

"Kylie, I'm glad I caught you." She noticed Landon and nodded to him.

Kylie made the introduction.

Landon shook Sadie's hand. "Ah, you're the mayor. I've heard good things about you."

Sadie winked at Kylie. "He's a good liar."

Kylie forced a smile.

"Hey, I wanted to let you know the city council voted to move to a bigger facility. I figured I'd let you know before we make it public."

"Wow. So soon."

"Well, you know how those slowpokes operate," Sadie said. "Nothing will be done for months."

Still, Kylie was in no way prepared. "Thanks, Sadie, I appreciate the heads-up."

"Think about it and let me know." Sadie turned to Landon. "You just passing through?"

He hesitated, then smiled. "I do have places to be."

"Well, nice meeting you."

Kylie waited until Sadie had stepped outside before she turned off the lights, hearing Landon's answer on a loop inside her head. It felt like everything was suddenly closing in on her.

As THEY WALKED to the truck, all Landon could think was that since they'd gotten back, every single thing had gone to hell in a handbasket.

It would help if Kylie could get more sleep, but dammit, he'd told Joe to show him the bill before he gave it to Kylie. And Joe had agreed. Stupid old buzzard. Landon wasn't quite as worried about Patty's revelation. Once

Kylie got some rest, she'd understand better. And now, the expansion option was more than just a maybe. *Shit*.

The short drive home was tense, and he hoped the surprise he had waiting for her would take care of that. He parked next to Barry's truck, counting on the kid's promise that he'd have everything finished.

He raised the garage door, keeping his eyes on Kylie. Her look of delight when she saw her new furniture made his heart start beating again.

She walked in slowly, right to the seats, smiling as she ran a hand down the distressed wood.

Landon breathed out a sigh of relief when she whispered, "Wow," at the tables that he'd made without anyone's help.

"It's all gorgeous. Better than I even imagined."

"There's still trim to add to the bench seats," Landon said. "Barry's idea. Thanks for finishing this up." Landon nodded at him. "Nice job."

She turned again to Barry, who was standing awkwardly next to a chair Landon hadn't seen before. It was a nifty design, compact, yet sturdy, that fit perfectly with the tables.

"What's this?" Kylie said, running her hand over the back of the chair. "Is it all right if I sit down?"

Barry nodded just as Landon said, "Of course."

"This is very comfortable." She leaned back. "But I probably wouldn't want to sit in it all day."

"Which makes it perfect," Landon said. "I think you'll find that's true for the bench seats as well."

When she stood, she turned to Landon. "I knew your brothers had to be teasing. You could do this professionally."

Barry let out a laugh that turned quickly into a cough.

Kylie glanced his way, a slight frown forming. "I

understand you were a terrific help. Thank you for all your hard work."

"You're welcome," he said.

She paused, still looking troubled, then pulled out her cell phone, and snapped several pictures. Including one of Barry backing up toward the door, his face flushed, and trying not to laugh again.

Landon closed his eyes, wanting to strangle the kid. Was every person in this town trying to sabotage him?

"He did all of the work, didn't he?" Kylie said, keeping her voice low.

"Not all of it." He met her eyes, and wished he hadn't. It would've been fine if his idiot brothers hadn't opened their big mouths.

"You lied to me. Again. You didn't ask Joe to order anything for your truck. Did you?" She blinked. "How much did all this cost, Landon?"

"Look, Kylie, I didn't mean to lie to you. I honestly thought I could do this myself, but then Chad convinced me that I wouldn't be up to the task. Which I saw for myself that first day. But I was embarrassed, okay? It was nothing more than my damn ego. Although I did distress the wood, and I built the tables on my own."

She kept staring at him with wounded eyes.

"I just wanted to make you happy."

After a sigh that was louder than Barry's truck backing up, her shoulders lowered. "I appreciate the thought, but it wasn't your place to do that, Landon. It's my business. My expenses. Which I'll pay for. I may not be able to pay it all right away, but I'll go to the bank tomorrow and—"

"Kylie, please—"

"If I can't get a loan, I'll set up a payment plan. I love the chair Barry built, but he needs to stop now. You need to stop."

"I understand." Landon felt as though his entire world was crumbling under his feet. A loan? Shit. "I'm sorry there were things I didn't take into consideration. You've worked hard for everything you've built, and I wouldn't want to take any of that away from you." He approached her slowly. "I just wanted to make you happy." He reached out to put his hands on her shoulders, but stopped before he touched her.

She nodded. "I know you meant well. Although I'm still confused about the motel…"

"I'll explain, I promise. But one thing you need to know. I paid Barry a bonus, but that was more about Barry than you. I wanted to give the kid and his family a hand. That's all on me, and nothing you need to worry about."

"That was good of you."

He pulled her close, relieved when she didn't resist.

"Landon? Just one more thing." She looked deeply into his eyes and there was no question she wasn't counting on the truth. "When are you leaving?"

"Physically, I'm ready to ride again. I realized that over the weekend," he admitted. "But I don't want to leave." Especially when they were on shaky ground.

"That doesn't answer my question."

He cupped her face. "Soon, sweetheart."

Before she could look any more disappointed, he swept her up in his arms, and took her straight through the house to the bedroom. At least he knew what he was doing in there.

Chapter Nineteen

"I'm sorry about the chairs. I'll talk to Kylie again and see what we can do, okay?"

Barry shrugged. "She seemed pretty pissed off yesterday."

"That she was." Landon held the strip of molding at the top of the first bench seat while Barry hammered in the penny nails.

At least she'd agreed they could put on the finishing touches. It bothered Landon to leave things like this with Barry, but he wasn't about to go behind Kylie's back again. His plan was to ask her if he could pay Barry to complete the work, and when it was convenient, she could pay him back.

If she brought up a bank loan again, then that was it. All work stopped. The thought of her getting into debt over this cut him off at the knees.

He hoped she'd say yes, for Barry's sake, sure, but if things went well, it would all be a moot point. The weekend with his family hadn't just told him he was ready to go back to the circuit, it had revealed something far more important. He'd made up his mind to ask Kylie to marry him.

Obviously, a few wrenches had been thrown in the works since he'd come to that decision. But once the dust settled and he wasn't so deep in the soup anymore he would ask her to be his wife. Kylie had a right to be angry, even though he'd already apologized. If it took a week of groveling, he'd do it. He was sure she'd come around. She wouldn't hold his stupidity against him forever.

After they'd made love—which had been more emotional, for him at least, than anything he'd experienced before—he'd spent most of last night thinking about his choices, and her reactions. Finally, it had gotten through his thick skull that she wasn't looking for a knight in shining armor. She didn't need someone to erase all the crap Gary had done to her. Kylie wanted independence and equal footing. He'd done far too little explaining and way too much assuming.

Tonight that would change. They were going to have a no-holds-barred talk.

"Uh, Landon?"

The molding had slipped. Now was not the time to get sloppy. He focused on the work, on making everything as perfect as they could before Barry packed up his things. Before Landon packed up *his* things.

His clock was running out.

This morning he'd made an appointment to see the orthopedic surgeon in Oklahoma before his next competition, then confirmed he was still in the lineups for four upcoming rodeos. Not that he hadn't been tempted to quit the whole damn thing. But he wanted the two of them—him and Kylie—to have a running start on the life he envisioned. Knowing he would pop the question before the finals made his resolve even stronger.

After Barry left, Landon spent the next hour cleaning up the garage, gathering the tools and equipment that would go back to Matt, and loaded what he could in the back of his truck. Then, he drove over to the motel.

Patty was at the reception desk. "Come to check out?"

He nodded, grateful that Kevin wasn't around. Not that it mattered. He'd know Landon had left soon enough.

"I'm sorry to see you leave," Patty said. "Especially after all you've done for Kylie."

"It was the least I could do," he said, glad that Patty didn't seem to know how much he'd screwed up in the doing department. "She's a wonderful woman."

"She sure is. I hope you come back after you win that gold buckle," Patty said. "You know we're all rooting for you."

"Thanks. Besides, I'm not that easy to get rid of."

Patty handed him the final accounting, and it was all over in a few minutes.

After returning Matt's stuff and buying him a beer, Landon parked near the bakery at almost four o'clock. Some kids who must've been close to Barry's age were laughing and talking as they headed toward Abe's Variety Store, and the twin old ladies who drove slow as molasses took their sweet time looking him over as they passed on the wrong side of the road.

The Cake Whisperer was crowded for this time of day, although he should've guessed everyone would want a gander at the new counter and to find out why she'd been closed. He'd been hoping Kylie would be ready to leave, but from the looks of things, she'd be a while.

She was busy boxing up something when he entered. Not wanting to bother her, he slipped into the kitchen, but he wasn't sure she noticed him.

The espresso machine was on the counter, along with a few bottled flavors and long stirrers, not much else, but the temptation to test it had obviously been too great. When he investigated, he realized there was hot water in the machine, and the manual was right there. He started to refresh himself on the operation, figuring he'd fix a coffee for himself and one for Kylie to go, but half-way down the second page, he heard Kevin's voice in the front.

It hadn't taken long at all for the news of his departure to spread.

Landon thought about ignoring the man, but since he was still trying to win points, Landon figured he'd be nice and make himself known. Kevin might really embarrass himself if he thought Landon had left town.

KYLIE HADN'T HAD such a busy day since her opening week. Celeste had helped this morning, but then her seven-year-old had fallen off the monkey bars, and Celeste had to go get her. Which left the entire population of Blackfoot Falls to stop by, order a donut or a cupcake and proceed to make a fuss over the new counters, and the much-discussed soon-to-open coffee bar. A lot of folks had a lot of opinions about that.

In the meantime, she was exhausted after a horrible night's sleep, and the last thing she needed was to deal with Kevin. Although, after their talk, she was surprised to see him here.

She handed Mrs. Tobin her bag of donuts and as she was ringing her up, Kevin said, "What are you doing here?" in a tone that was less than friendly. "I figured you were on your way to Texas."

Kylie turned to find Landon standing about two feet behind her. He smiled at her, then turned his grin on Kevin. "So you follow the circuit, do you? Just broncs or…?"

"I like to keep up. And from what I hear, you'll need to ride a lot if you want to stay ranked."

"That's true. I will. But I'll make up for it."

Kevin didn't look all that happy. Which wasn't her problem.

"I'll bet you don't have any trouble, Kincaid," came a low voice from near the window. "I saw you ride in Wyoming last spring, and damn you have some slick moves."

Kylie hadn't even seen Rudy, a lanky cowboy who was a semi-regular, come in, his jeans sending out clouds of dust as he approached the counter.

"Hey, thanks. But there's no guarantees." He shrugged. "It's not just slick moves. Sometimes the horse wins."

That brought a laugh from some of the ladies, especially the two women from the Sundance who were checking out Landon like he was a juicy steak.

"I know you're scheduled to ride in Dallas in a week and then Albuquerque after that. You gonna make it?"

"I have to if I want to make the finals."

A box of cupcakes almost slipped out of Kylie's hands.

Last night she'd flat out asked when he was leaving. And all he did was pull another one of his *slick moves*. Was he incapable or just unwilling to tell her anything?

With the heat of fury coursing through her, she continued to serve her customers. She managed to be somewhat pleasant, but it wasn't easy. At least Kevin got the hint and left without saying a word to her. All she wanted was for *everyone* to go away. Leave her alone. Stop talking about the rodeo or for heaven's sake, caramel coffee lattes!

The moment the last customer walked out the door, she had the Closed sign out and the door locked. She zeroed in on Landon, and the smile he'd worn disappeared like icing on a hot cake.

"What a day, huh?" he said. "If I help you clean the kitchen do you think we can go over to the steakhouse for dinner and to talk?"

"About?"

"My schedule, for one thing. And also about Barry."

"Your schedule, as in when you'll be leaving?"

He nodded, his face creased in confusion.

Join the club.

"Look, I made a few calls this morning. I needed an appointment with my doctor before I took off for Texas, and then I had to make sure I was still on the marquee—"

"How convenient."

"I don't follow," he said slowly.

"I don't care." She was spitting mad. "What I don't understand is why you're still here at all. If you need to go, go. Leave now. Clearly you're not staying on my account." She whipped off her apron and rolled it into a tight little ball. "You said right from the start you were only here temporarily. It's probably the only honest thing you've said to me, so just…go. Leave already."

He seemed stunned. And hurt. But that wasn't her fault. Not after all he'd pulled.

"I came to tell you the plan—"

"Sure, after Kevin and Rudy forced your hand."

"What are you talking about?"

He didn't look guilty or defensive, just confused. While she would probably never sleep again worrying about all the money she owed.

"Look…" He held his hand out. "I wasn't trying to hide anything from you. I only made the decision about when to get back on the circuit today. After my phone calls."

Behind her someone banged on the door, then on the window. Kylie wanted to just scream, not even sure she trusted herself to be polite.

"Um, you might want to get that," Landon said. "She can see us. It's Shirley."

Kylie stiffened. Her entire chest twisted into a painful knot. "Shirley?" she whispered. She'd never fainted before, but it was possible she would now… "The birthday cake. Oh, my God."

Landon's mouth tightened. "Did you forget?"

She was supposed to have made it this morning. After Celeste left. "Get out," she said calmly.

"Kylie…"

"Right now."

He didn't move.

"My life was really good here, Landon," she murmured, tears filling her eyes. "Until you came and screwed up everything."

"Let's talk to her. I'll help. We can still make the cake—"

"You call yourself my friend. What crap! You were never my friend. You could've told me about Gary's cheating, but you didn't. You just let me be humiliated. And you think everything can be solved by sex. So like him. So like *him*."

"Come on, that's not fair." Anger stained his face. "Last night wasn't about trying to slip something by you. And as for Gary, you know I couldn't say anything."

"Bull."

"You think I wasn't tempted? You wouldn't have believed me. I wanted you for myself and you knew it. I would've loved to see you dump his ass."

Shirley banged on the window again.

Kylie ignored her. Almost too sick and angry to speak, she held Landon's gaze. "You're a liar. Just like Gary. Wanna deny that?" She paused. "No? Then go," she said, swallowing thickly. "Just go."

They stared at each other for a charged moment. "Fine." He tossed the espresso instructions on the counter. "But don't kid yourself. No one had to tell you about Gary. The signs were all there but you didn't want to face it. You had to catch him in the act. Tell me, whose fault was that?"

He brushed past her, angrier than she'd ever seen him. From what she could make out through her tears, anyway.

TWO WEEKS LATER, Kylie came home after working thirteen hours and decided to clean the house. She was exhausted. Nothing new there. She actually functioned better when she was too tired to think. Ask anyone in town. Just about everyone had an opinion about her mood lately. And an opinion about Landon. And what had happened to make him leave. If she wasn't so depressed she might've found the varying accounts entertaining.

However, if one more person asked her when she was going to set up the espresso machine, she'd hurl the damn thing through the window. Let it sit in the middle of Main Street. Then they could all make their own drinks.

She pulled her ancient vacuum out of the closet and even before she plugged it in she could tell from the poufs of dust that the bag needed changing. A chore she hated more than anything. She should've made Landon do it.

See? Using her brain at all wasn't a good idea. She seemed to keep circling back to him.

Even though she'd cleaned the small house from top to bottom twice since he'd left, she still hadn't been able to get rid of his scent. Or shake the sense that he was going to sneak up behind her at any moment and kiss her neck.

How could she miss him so much? He'd gone behind her back, manipulated the truth. Hidden important things from her.

She was right to be furious. And yet that hadn't

stopped her from thinking about him. Or about her own part in this mess.

It had taken a couple of days, but she'd finally understood why he hadn't told her about Gary's cheating.

She *had* known, back then. About the other women. About her feelings for Landon that she'd tried to hide. From Gary, at least, as she tried so hard to save what was already ruined.

The bitter irony was how afraid she'd been of turning out like her mother and yet she hadn't even seen that staying with Gary was Darlene all over.

At least Landon had been clearheaded enough to leave her be after they'd almost— Come to think of it, maybe if they'd actually kissed, things would have turned out better.

In the end, though, it hadn't made a difference.

She wiped her cheek with the back of her hand then hauled the vacuum out to the garage. The moment she turned on the light she wanted to go right back inside.

The beautifully aged ash benches, the tables, perfectly balanced for holding hot coffees. And of course the one lone chair that would chase even Goldilocks out of the bakery after an hour.

Everything was ready to be loaded up and taken to The Cake Whisperer. She'd had offers of help from Matt and Gunner. Even Kevin said he'd rent a truck. But her enthusiasm for the coffee bar had cooled so much that the only reason they were using the espresso machine at all was because Celeste insisted.

Even without the tables and chairs, there was enough milling about by the busybodies to make her days more hectic. And aggravating.

Everyone seemed to have known about Landon's *surprise*, and how worried he'd been about pulling it off. She knew for a fact he didn't personally know half the people that acted as if they were his best pals. Word had spread like a virus. The women thought Landon was the most romantic cowboy that had ever mounted a horse. While the men grumbled he'd raised the damn bar too high and their wives would never give them any peace again.

But they didn't know everything.

They didn't know he'd toyed with her about his future plans. She still had no idea where he expected to end up, and she'd bet his family didn't know either. There was so much she'd ignored, even though he'd said he wasn't sure about things. She had no right to be shocked now that the blinders were off.

She felt so stupid.

Thinking about it was enough to get her to change the damn vacuum bag, but as she struggled to make it fit, Rachel phoned.

"Has he called?" Rachel asked.

"No. And I haven't called him." This was getting really old. "When are you going to stop asking?"

"When you get your head out of your butt."

"Oh, is that how we're playing it?" Kylie was starting to move past irritated. Wasn't Rachel supposed to be on her side? "Go have a brownie. Hell, I've got a chocolate torte sitting in the fridge. Have at it."

Rachel gasped. "That does it. We need to have a talk. You, me and the girls. And I mean now."

"Pass."

"We'll be there in forty minutes."

"I'll leave."

"I'll sic Grace on you."

Kylie sighed. "I need new friends."

Rachel simply laughed as she disconnected.

Chapter Twenty

What another stinker of a day. Thank God it was Saturday. Kylie couldn't wait to get home, lock the doors and not have to speak to another living soul.

Kylie would've been worried about making it home without crying again, but she had no tears left after hearing from the bank. They weren't going to approve her loan.

Just as she was crossing Main Street, she thought she saw Landon's truck a block away. Great. Now she was imagining things. Clearly it couldn't be him, since he was back on the circuit, but she'd never seen another maroon color like it around town. Why would he be here, anyway? Apparently, neither of them had wanted to be the first to call, so they hadn't spoken since that last nightmarish day.

Even though she'd let go of her anger, she was still disappointed that Landon had left so many questions unanswered. But even more disappointed in herself. She'd been right to want to give them a real chance, but she'd been oh, so foolish to ignore reality. She could have asked him, and told him what worked for her and what didn't work, but she hadn't. She tried to blame it on fear, after her experience with Gary, but it wasn't that. It was her being a child. She might have built a business by herself, but a healthy relationship had been beyond her.

As the truck came closer she couldn't help but look to see who was driving.

She froze in the street, one foot on the sidewalk.

Landon?

As he drove past her, he lifted a hand in a casual wave, as if it hadn't been three weeks since they'd seen each other. As if they were still friends.

He didn't stop, just kept driving.

She watched him park in front of the Watering Hole and told herself whatever he was doing here, it had nothing to do with her. Somehow her feet didn't get the message.

Keeping her eyes trained on him, she picked up the pace, her heart pounding so fast she could scarcely breathe. Rachel better not have anything to do with this, her or her merry band of annoying culprits.

Landon didn't get out of the truck right away. If he was waiting for her, well, she... She had no idea what she was going to do.

Just as she reached the bed of the truck, he opened the door and climbed out, his gaze immediately finding hers. At least he didn't try to pretend he hadn't seen her.

She stopped several feet away. He needed a shave and a week of solid sleep by the look of those shadows under his eyes. As if she should talk. Except Landon had pulled the brim of his Stetson down low, and even tired, he looked too damn handsome. While she was a big puffy mess.

"Hello, Kylie," he said, and took off the hat.

"What are you doing here?"

He stared uneasily at her. "I have some business to take care of."

"Business?"

"I'd also like to speak with you if you'll give me a chance to explain a few things."

"Aren't you supposed to be in Kansas City about now?" she asked, and when his eyes narrowed slightly, she realized how much she'd just told him. She looked down at his boots. "Did you hurt your leg again?"

"No," he said. "The leg's fine. The rest of me isn't so hot." He gave her that lopsided smile. "I miss you, Kylie."

She drew in a shaky breath and glanced around. People were staring. She met Landon's intense gaze and lowered her voice. "Why are you really here?"

"Business, like I said. And for you."

Trying to swallow was useless. "You didn't even call."

"You didn't want me to."

"Really?" Kylie needed to make sure he wasn't playing games. "How would you know that?"

"I know because you're a strong, independent woman, who wouldn't put up with my crap, or anyone else's. And you had every right to be angry with me." He paused and glanced around at the crowd they'd attracted. "Can we sit in the truck?"

For moment, she let all he'd said sink in. Before she jumped him for being wonderful, she said, "What about your business appointment?"

He actually checked his watch. "I still have ten minutes."

Huh. He really had an appointment? Well, it wasn't much time for her to do her own explaining. "Fine," she said and walked around to the passenger side.

He joined her in the cab, making sure all the windows were up, and she almost laughed at the disappointed faces around them.

"Okay," she said. "You think you know me so well. Why would I want to talk to you now?"

"You're a fair-minded person. You'll hear me out. Even if you don't like what I have to say. Which makes me a bigger ass for not talking to you sooner."

Damn him. "Go on."

"I was dead wrong sneaking behind your back, no matter what my intentions. But I don't think we need to rehash things in that department. Lord knows we have enough to discuss."

She shifted nervously. They did?

"Look, Kylie, I'm not using this as an excuse, I swear I'm not. But I felt trapped—"

"Oh, my God, you don't get to say that. I never asked you for any—"

He took her hand, startling her into silence. "Let me finish. Actually, I should start from the beginning. Before I came here. Initially, I told my family I was moving back home to work with Chad and Martin. Honestly, that's all I'd ever wanted. But as time went on I started to realize what a risk we'd all be taking. You said it yourself, Chad had grabbed life by the tail. It wasn't easy for him to step up and make himself useful.

"I couldn't take that away from him. If I went back, all of a sudden he wouldn't have as much responsibility to shoulder. I couldn't let him slip back into that dark hole again. Tell me I'm being manipulative or sneaky, whatever, but I wasn't willing to take that chance."

He glanced away and cleared his throat. "So about six months ago I told them I wanted to spread my wings, run my own operation. Of course, Chad gave me shit about being a cocky rodeo star and if that's what he wanted to think, I was fine with that. When I said I'd find a place nearby, Martin razzed me about staying close to the nest."

Landon shrugged, stared at something on the hood. "That was okay, too. In a way it was the truth. I love my family, and I'd wanted to live as close as I could, watch Liam, Fiona and Jenna grow up. Be there if they needed help. So it was a good solution.

"Until I came here and I fell in love with you."

Kylie was relieved she was already sitting down.

He touched her arm. "I'm not saying that was a bad thing. Those two weeks we spent together was the happiest time of my life. But it turned out to be more complicated the longer I was here. That's when I started feeling trapped, knowing what my family expected." He squeezed her hand, his gaze steady as he looked deep into her eyes. "Kylie, I see how much people care about you here. You've made great friends. You have the bakery. Hell, in one year you've put down roots. That's a rare thing. I would never ask you to move to Wyoming, leave everything you've built behind.

"So, that's why I'm here telling you things I should have spelled out long ago." He glanced at his watch again. "In three minutes I'm meeting with a Realtor. She's going to show me three ranches between here and Kalispell. Hell, it's only six hours to the Running Bear. And then, later, I'm going to ask you to be my wife. You'll say no, and so I'll ask you again in two weeks. And then again two weeks later. You know what a stubborn jackass I am."

Kylie laughed. It was that, or cry buckets.

"You know, you can talk now." He looked endearingly nervous, searching her face, squeezing her hand a little too tight.

She drew a shaky breath. "I have more than three minutes of apologies to make."

"What?"

"It wasn't just that you didn't tell me everything. I

spent all our time together not wanting to have things spelled out. I didn't know if I could take it. Those two weeks were the best I ever had, too. I didn't want reality to ruin anything. So I kept letting it ride. I'm sorry."

"I think we might have both been on that horse."

"Speaking of horses, aren't you supposed to ride this weekend?"

"I am, but I also know you're not crazy about that. Plus, it'll keep us apart. I don't mind admitting, these last three weeks have been hell without you. I needed to know exactly where we stood. So…it was simple. I decided to come here and find out."

She touched his face. Liar. Sweet, sweet liar. She could feel his tension, see the struggle in his eyes. Oh, she believed he'd chosen her over the rodeo, but there had been nothing simple about that decision. "How are you going to the finals if you aren't ranked, you dope?"

His Adam's apple bobbed as he swallowed. "What are you saying?"

"That you need to win the million bucks to pay for my chairs and espresso machine."

He started to laugh.

"Oh, and yes."

And he stopped laughing just as quickly. "Kylie…"

"I love you, too. And yes, I'll marry you. So we can start a ranch together after you're ready to leave the rodeo. And also so you don't have to pester me every two weeks." She blinked back the tears. "By the way, you can't drive and make it in time. Kalispell has an airport. As for the Realtor—"

He kissed her so hard she fell back against the seat. Clutching his shoulders, she kissed him back. How in this crazy world had she gotten so lucky?

When they came up for air, he gave her that lopsided

grin she loved. "Let me tell the Realtor to put the appointment on hold, and then we can drive out to the airport. You take my truck back, and I'll manage from there."

"Then I'll meet you in Vegas for the finals."

His grin somehow grew. "You mean it?"

"I already ordered my ticket."

He gave her an adorable frown. "You know, you could've led with that."

Kylie laughed. "Go on, hurry up. We've got a great big future to start."

* * * * *

*If you enjoyed this story, check out more
great ranching romances available now from
Harlequin Western Romance.
New families are created in Marie Ferrarella's
TWINS ON THE DOORSTEP and
Mary Leo's A BABY FOR THE SHERIFF.
And a single mom finds love in Roz Denny Fox's
MARRYING THE RANCHER.*

♦H HARLEQUIN®

Western Romance

Available November 7, 2017

#1665 A TEXAS SOLDIER'S CHRISTMAS

Texas Legacies: The Lockharts
by Cathy Gillen Thacker

Soldier Zane Lockhart rushes home to Texas to claim his son, then discovers Nora Caldwell's adopted baby isn't his. He still wants to make the army nurse and her boy family—in time for baby Liam's first Christmas!

#1666 THE COWBOY SEAL'S CHRISTMAS BABY

Cowboy SEALs • by Laura Marie Altom

When former navy SEAL Gideon Snow finds a baby and a woman with amnesia on a remote Arizona trail, he's forced to take them home. Christmas at his ranch just got more interesting!

#1667 A SNOWBOUND COWBOY CHRISTMAS

Saddle Ridge, Montana • by Amanda Renee

Single mom-to-be Emma Sheridan has one job: convince Dylan Slade to sell his Montana guest ranch. But when Emma is stuck in Saddle Ridge, she realizes she likes being snowbound with the handsome rancher.

#1668 THE BULL RIDER'S PLAN

Montana Bull Riders • by Jeannie Watt

Jess Hayward is off on a rodeo road trip, where he plans to fulfill his bull-riding dream. But he doesn't expect Emma Sullivan, his best friend's sister, to tag along. She's a distraction he doesn't need!

HWESTCNM1017

Get 2 Free Books,

HARLEQUIN®
Western Romance

Plus 2 Free Gifts—
just for trying the Reader Service!

Looking for more satisfying love stories
with community and family at their core?

**Check out Harlequin® Special Edition
and Harlequin® Western Romance** books!

New books available every month!

***

CONNECT WITH US AT:

Harlequin.com/Community

ReaderService.com

HARLEQUIN®

**ROMANCE WHEN
YOU NEED IT**

HFGENRE2017R